THE MEMORY THIEF

THE MEMORY THIEF

BRYCE MOORE

ADAPTIVE BOOKS

An Imprint of Adaptive Studios
Culver City, CA

Copyright © 2016 Bryce Moore

Visit us on the web at www.adaptivestudios.com

Library of Congress Cataloging-in-Publication Number: 2016943461
ISBN 978-0-9964887-7-8
Printed in the United States of America.
Designed by Torborg Davern Design

Adaptive Books
3578 Hayden Avenue, Suite 6
Culver City, CA 90232

10 9 8 7 6 5 4 3 2 1

Also by

BRYCE MOORE

VODNÍK

For Tomas, the best son a dad could ask for.

THE FAIR

My parents were fighting. Again.

It wasn't at home, either. Fighting at home was normal. Out in public, they tried to pretend everything was fine. Happy Mom, happy Dad, two happy children. They would wait for the front door to close before they went at it, except when things were really bad.

Public fight in the middle of the county fair?

Really bad.

I stared at another shelf of onions and potatoes, my hands shoved down my pockets and my shoulders hunched. The exhibit hall ran a hundred yards along the side of the fairgrounds, the first level filled with booths and shelves stocked with the cream of the crop for Adams County, Maine. Peppers. Dill. Carrots! Ugh.

While outside was a nice brisk September evening, the inside of the hall was stuffy and cramped. Or maybe my parents just made it feel that way. My twin sister, Kelly, stood next to me, eyes glued to her video game. If I hadn't forgotten mine at home, I could have at least been playing against her.

Kelly didn't look too much like me, of course. We were fraternal twins, not identical. So where I had dark brown hair that I kept cut short, Kelly had long dark curls in a loose ponytail. My nose was bigger, but she was two inches taller than me. Two and a half, tops.

An older couple walked past us, giving the argument plenty of space. The ancient floorboards creaked in protest with each step.

"Don't give me any of that, Ford." It wasn't a full-blown yell from my mom. That would have been better. This was a tight hiss of frustration. "I worked the whole day getting things—"

"Worked," Dad shot back in the same tone. "Please, Zoe. I'd die for your job. Stay at home while the kids are at school? You don't even—"

The argument hadn't started with Mom being a stay-at-home mother, but it always led there eventually. I tried to tune out the bickering, focusing instead on figuring out how many different types of canned fruit the Wilton Grange had come up with this year.

Kelly glanced up from her game, judged the situation, and jerked her head up toward the second floor. "Wanna go upstairs?" she mouthed at me.

I nodded, glancing at our parents. We might as well have not even existed. A few more people walking past gave them uneasy looks. My face flushed in embarrassment.

Kelly and I feigned interest in some flower arrangements down the hall, sidestepping our way until we were far enough to just leave altogether, heading for the second-floor exhibits. Arts and crafts. You could enter anything handmade that year into the fair competition. The winners got colored ribbons and a few bucks. That had been exciting four or five years ago. To twelve-year-olds, it wasn't nearly as thrilling. Mom still made us enter.

Then again, it was "not where my parents are arguing," so it might as well have been paradise.

I kept a lookout for other kids from school, mainly to avoid the ones I didn't want to see. You had to be aware of things like that. The coast was clear for now.

The second floor was a mirror of the first: two long rows of displays running the length of the building, just with pictures and paintings lining the walls instead of flowers and vegetables. The middle of the hall had display cases full of handmade items ranging from jellies to skirts. The air was even muggier up here, and the floorboards squeaked just as loudly.

"Do you think you won anything?" Kelly asked, peeking up from her game long enough to make sure she wasn't about to run into anyone.

I shrugged. "It gets harder the older you are."

She stopped playing and looked at me. "If you'd practice carving as much as you complained about how hard it was, you'd get first every year."

I walked over to the craft section. My horse had tipped on its side in the glass case. I wanted to reach in and rebalance it. If you placed it just right, it stayed put. I'd tried to explain that when I dropped it off, but apparently they hadn't gotten the message.

A blue ribbon sat next to a carved and painted loon. The craftsman had gotten everything perfect, right down to the texture of the individual feathers.

My horse was ribbon-free.

I reached into my pocket and put my hand around the pocketknife I'd gotten for Christmas four years ago. The red covering was smooth and cool against my fingers, the knife and attachments bumpy but familiar. It had taken me four times to come up with something I thought might be ribbon-worthy. If you looked at the horse from the right angle, it was pretty decent. One of his legs was the wrong length, though. I'd slipped while trying to get the details of the hooves right. Experience had taught me not to try fixing the other legs to make them the same length. I'd done that before and ended up with a fat dog instead of a horse.

It was too difficult, even though I'd read a ton of books about it. Maybe it was because I was always scared I was going to cut myself, and that made me too worried about the blade to really *use* it right. I wished I could just pay somebody to download "How to Be a Woodcarver" right into my brain.

Kelly's arm went around my shoulders. "It's okay," she said. "There's always next year. It's not like that rose Mom made me cross-stitch did any better. It turned out more like a picture of a wounded Jell-O mold." She'd put away her game. With our parents downstairs arguing, she didn't need to ignore what was happening around her.

"I thought you guys were twins, not boyfriend/girlfriend," a voice spoke with a snigger, farther back.

Three guys from school had come out from behind one of the quilt displays that lined the center of the hall. Matt Jones, Michael Stinson, and Sam Hyde. My school's resident trolls. I glanced up and down the room. We were alone. Not even a pair of senior citizens eyeing up the knitting work. I tried to pull away, but Kelly kept her arm around my shoulder, hugging me tighter. "It's called family affection," she said. "You guys have probably never heard of it."

"Kelly," I muttered, embarrassed.

"Kelly," Sam mimicked. The kid had the creativity of a slug. A slug that couldn't pass art.

Kelly took her arm from around my shoulders, balled her hand into a fist, and tried to take a few steps forward. I held her back, and she settled for a simple glare. "Don't you have a rock you're supposed to go crawl under, Sam?"

The smile drained from his face. Maybe he'd been joking before—mostly—but he hadn't expected Kelly to insult him like that in front of his friends. My sister was always the doer. The one who wouldn't back down from a challenge. She was always telling me I needed to stand up for myself better.

"What did you say to me?" Sam asked.

Kelly started to respond, but I elbowed her. "Come on, guys," I said. "Leave us alone?"

Michael took this as his cue to chime in as head toady to Sam. "Not until she apologizes."

My sister frowned. "For what?"

"For talking back," Matt piped up, not one to be left behind by Michael.

"You want back talk?" Kelly said, shaking off my arm. "How about I—"

A new voice spoke from behind us. "Benjamin Clive and Kelly Joy Lewis."

Mom and Dad had found us. And they might have been arguing before, but whenever we made them mad, they usually found common ground long enough to punish us. They stood there, hands on hips, in front of the children's art competition.

"What?" I asked. Sam and his friends melted away. And maybe there was an edge to my voice, but I was upset at the confrontation with Sam and angry at my parents, and they deserved to know it.

Mom's lips were a thin line. "Who said you could come up here by yourselves?"

"You're the ones who were too busy yelling at each other to notice," I said. "Don't take it out on me because you feel guilty."

Dad pointed a finger at me. "Don't talk to your mother that way."

Normally, I would have backed down, but not today. All the tension from the afternoon—the anticipation of having fun at the fair, the disappointment when I realized my parents were fighting and it was going to be one of "those" evenings instead, the embarrassment of having them do it in public—it all came boiling out.

"What, Dad? You mean you're the only one who gets to

yell at her? I thought we came here to go on rides, not to talk about money and jobs. You guys can be such—such—*jerks*." There must have been a better word than that, but I could never come up with the right thing to say when I was mad.

Dad's face turned red with anger. Mom just paled.

"Go," Kelly whispered. "I got this."

Go? Go where? But all I wanted was to be away from the fighting. Away from the worries. And Kelly could calm them down. Maybe. I felt bad about it. I was ruining her evening just like Mom and Dad. But we often took a tag-team approach to problems. I turned and strode down the hall toward the exit at the far end, the door outlined by the bright light of the setting sun.

"Benjamin!" Dad called out.

I kept walking.

"Ben!" That was Mom.

If they wanted me so badly, they could come and stop me. But they didn't.

I made it out the door and down the rickety staircase outside before I glanced behind me.

No one was there. Had they let me go? I looked around. People swarmed everywhere, just like every discount night. Old guys with huge bellies, women talking on cell phones, high schoolers making out or holding hands. All of them strangers. Livingston was a small town, and I always felt like

I knew everyone—until fair week rolled around.

I looked back at the exhibit hall again, expecting one of my parents to be there glaring at me. The door was still empty. I could go back. Tell them I was sorry and try to salvage some of the evening. But what's the point in making a stand if you sat down right after?

Let Mom and Dad worry about something other than being mad at each other for once. And besides, with all these people around, it wasn't like anything bad was going to happen to me. I dove into the crowd.

Things went well at first. I had some money I'd saved up, and the smell of fried dough and grilling meat was too much not to get *something*. That something turned into fries, an ICEE, and a doughboy very quickly. I checked out the maple-sugar shack and spent my last few dollars on maple cotton candy. I had a general plan in mind: waste time until the Demolition Derby at seven. It was grown-up bumper cars, with people driving into each other head-on. Two years ago, one of the cars drove right over one of the others and then flipped on its roof, and I had high hopes for a repeat performance.

I'd worry about finding my parents and Kelly after it was over.

My plan fell apart by the blacksmith's shop. I'd been watching him pound away at iron, his face red and sweaty, the iron bending slowly underneath his blows. It sounded like someone pummeling a muted bell. I couldn't figure out what he was making, and before I could, someone bumped into me from behind, hard.

Sam. And he wasn't alone.

I took one glance over my shoulder—enough to confirm who it was—and sped off into the exhibit hall next to the smith. Fighting Sam one-on-one would have been possible. With his two goons? Forget it.

The chase was epic. We sprinted past the Gravitron and the vomit comet, through the cow stalls and the bird pens, weaving between people and animals alike. In a flat-out race, I would have been in trouble. Sam, Michael, and Matt played sports. I didn't. But this wasn't just a race. It was more like "Full-Contact Hide-and-Seek."

And I was great at hiding.

I caught a glimpse of Mom and Dad through the crowd when I was hunched under a picnic table by the Sausage Shack, catching my breath. They weren't fighting anymore; their faces wore the same expression of concern and worry. Kelly was trailing along behind them, playing her game. I thought she was lost in concentration, but she took a moment to glance up at me and stick out her tongue. People thought she was oblivious when she was playing her games. She wasn't.

I put my finger to my lips and shook my head. Maybe if my parents stopped focusing on hating each other for a second, they'd forget they didn't get along. And Sam and his cronies hadn't caught me yet. Better the possibility of impending doom than the certainty of what would happen when my parents found me. Kelly nodded, then glanced up at Mom and Dad and pointed off in the opposite direction.

Twins were the best.

Michael found my hiding spot, and I had to burst out, cutting across the back side of some of the rides to get away. The path was littered with cables, and I almost tripped twice. My pulse roared in my ears, and my breath started to get ragged, but I escaped again. The adults ignored us or yelled at us. Just a bunch of overexcited kids at the fair.

I would lose the bullies in the crowd, but they were like a pack of wolves that had caught the scent of blood, and the fair was only so big.

The chase was closing in, driving me toward the stadium. On that edge of the fair, the tone shifted. There were more stores: run-down booths with people hawking everything from T-shirts to religion—places I didn't feel comfortable darting into and hiding. At the first one I tried—selling everything you could think of, as long as it was made out of leather—the owner hollered at me as soon as I ducked under the table.

Matt heard the commotion and yelled for his buddies. I ran out the back of the booth and circled around toward friendlier territory: a woman selling fudge. But as I emerged from her display, bumping hard into a table and making the fudge stacks wobble, the others were almost on top of me, with Sam in the lead.

I streaked off toward the stadium, hoping I'd be able to lose them among the crowd that was forming for the derby. Sweat streamed down my face, even in the chill evening air. The stadium was only twenty-five yards off, but halfway there, I saw Matt had gotten there first.

Where else could I go?

Down at the end, almost to the stadium itself, sat a lone circus tent. Not a big one, obviously. More like a circus tent in miniature. Stripes of green, purple, and white ran down its sides, and a little overhang of the same fabric jutted out in front, with a few round paper lanterns casting it all in an orange light. I'd never seen it at the fair before. If I could get in there, maybe the rest of them would follow. I'd be cornered, but wild thoughts ran through my mind: me using my pocketknife to slice open the tent and get free of everyone, or knocking the tent down and escaping in the chaos that ensued. That always worked in cartoons.

It was that or nothing.

I noticed a sign out front as I pounded past it:

THE MEMORY EMPORIUM
MEMORIES BOUGHT AND SOLD

I dashed up to the overhang, ripped aside the sheet of cloth covering the entrance, and dove inside.

CHAPTER

2

LOUIS

Candles illuminated the inside of the tent, which was much smaller than I thought it would be based on the outside. Cheap incense filled the room with a smell like pine trees coated in sweaty socks, with more than a hint of body odor. Then again, the BO might have been coming from the old man passed out at the table in the middle of the tent.

Only the slight snores and the spreading puddle of drool by his mouth assured me he wasn't dead. He wore a bulky suit that made his slight build look like a turtle that might go back in its shell at any moment. A plaid golf cap sat on the table next to him.

Sam barged in, the tent flap whipping through the air and interrupting the peace of the tent. He almost ran into me. Sam glanced at the old guy, then tapped me on the shoulder.

"You," he whispered. "Outside. Now."

"No," I said back in a normal voice.

He slugged me in the shoulder, and a jolt of pain shot down my whole arm.

"Ow!" I shouted. How deaf was that old guy? Was it too much to hope he would wake up and save me?

For once, I got lucky. The man bolted up.

"Customers!" he shouted.

Sam and I took a step back in unison, surprised.

The man stared each of us in the eye. "Sam. You were just leaving, weren't you? And take those hoodlums outside my door with you. I need to talk to Benjamin."

I'd never seen this man before in my life, but he knew my name? Sam turned and left, a bewildered look on his face, like he was confused how he got there to begin with.

The old man kept staring at me. His eyes seemed too big for his face, and he was even frailer than I'd thought at first, his teeth yellowed and his eyes cloudy. "Welcome to my tent!" he said, then tried to stand. He got about halfway up and couldn't make it the rest of the way.

"Hey," I said. "What just . . ." I glanced behind me at the flap.

"How can I help you, Benji?" the man asked.

I frowned. "Do I know you?"

He shook his head. "But I know you. Know you better than you know yourself, I'd wager. Allow me to introduce myself. My name is Louis, Memory Artist extraordinaire." He made a little flourish with his hand. "Please sit," he said.

"Oh," I said, taking the chair in front of the table and feeling like I was at the principal's office. My pulse was slowing down, and I had caught my breath. Outside, an announcement blared over the loudspeaker, letting everyone know the Demolition Derby would begin in thirty minutes. "Thanks. I'm . . . uh . . . Benji. Benjamin." But he had known that already. How?

Louis straightened his red tie, clapped his hands together, and smiled. "Well, Benjamin. As I said, I am a Memory Artist. Dealer of Yesteryear. Borrower of the Past." He hitched his pants up, despite the fact that they were already well on their way to his chest. They had a tendency to droop, even when he was sitting.

"What does that mean?" I asked. "Do you, like . . . want me to tell you about stuff that's happened to me?"

Louis shook his head. "Of course not, my boy. I take unwanted memories. Buy them, actually. Lift them right out of your head." He snapped his fingers. Or tried to. "Just like that."

I frowned again. "What?"

"You ever had a bad nightmare you wish you could forget? I can make you forget it. Nightmares, lost loves, failed dreams, embarrassing situations. I take 'em all. For cash. Those don't get you much, of course. I pay more for better things. Memories you might like but aren't using. Winning the spelling bee. Your first steps. Things you don't even know you've got stored up there, although maybe you're still competing in spelling bees, yes?"

I sat back in my chair as far as I could go. Was he crazy?

"I'm *not* crazy," he proclaimed, perhaps more loudly than he intended to.

"Can you read minds?" I blurted out.

He shrugged. "In a manner of speaking. I can read memories. I can't tell what you're thinking until after you've thought it."

"But . . . how?"

Louis spread his arms. "I told you, my boy. I'm a Memory Artist."

Whatever that was. "I haven't seen you at the fair before."

"I haven't been here, but if I had, you wouldn't remember me unless I wanted you to. I'm looking for someone, and I just got here today. Have you seen a woman with tattoos up and down her arms? Or a group of RVs all traveling together?"

I picked at the edge of my chair. It was wood that had seen years of use. "I've seen a lot of women, and a lot of tattoos. I haven't paid any attention to RVs. It's fair week. They're all over the place." What a strange question.

"She looks young. Well, younger than me, but who isn't? Twenty years old. Short brown hair. And tattoos that are . . . singular."

"No," I said. "I haven't seen her."

"If you do, stay away! Come find me. Will you do that?"

I nodded.

He stared at me and then smiled. "I believe you will. You're a good boy, Benjamin. And I'm sorry about your parents. They'll get over it, though. It really comes down to money, not love."

"Okay," I said, having had enough. "That is too strange. Were you following me?"

Louis considered before continuing. "Maybe this would make more sense if I showed you something. I can *give* memories, too. The first one's on me. Free of charge." He smiled even wider, showing a mouth full of dentures, and held his hand out to me across the table. "Now," he said. "Give me your hand."

What did I have to lose? I reached to take his hand. When I was inches away, he drew back, staring at me with his eyes narrowed, as if he was considering something. He made up his mind about whatever it was and shook my hand. His skin was leathery and rough.

I was in a plane, the roar of the engines drowning out everything else. This wasn't a passenger plane. Seats lined the edges of the cabin, and a green light cast a shadowy glow on everything. Fifty other people—men—sat with me, dressed in olive-green cargo pants and jackets, round helmets with webbing on them, big brown boots, and parachutes on their backs.

On my back, too.

The plane shook with turbulence and the buzz of the engines. This wasn't like a movie. This was real. As real as the fair had been moments before. I could feel the texture of my uniform. The scratchiness around the collar. Smell the fuel oil, sweat, and exhaust. My body was bigger. Older. More muscled. And I didn't have any control over it. I was a spectator—watching and experiencing what it did, but unable to influence it.

Some of the other guys on the plane were praying, their lips moving silently. From over the roar of the plane's engines, I thought I heard the ratatat of machine gun fire. Then a loud explosion.

The plane hit a patch of rough air and dropped a hundred feet. My stomach flew up into my mouth, and I felt sick. An older man strode to a door and flung it open. The cabin filled with the swoosh *of air.*

A red light started flashing, and we all stood and headed for the door, jumping out one by one.

I wanted to stop. Head back to my seat. But of course my body didn't listen. There were still five guys between me, leaping out into nothing. What would it be like? How had I gotten here? Four guys. Three.

It might not have been my body, but it was nervous. My palms were sweaty, and my mouth was dry as cotton. The guy in front of me hurled himself through the door without a pause, and then it was my turn.

I thought I'd stop. Refuse to jump. I was terrified, after all. My feet were inches from nothingness. It was dark out. The wind whipped through my hair, threatening to pull off my helmet, except it was strapped tight over my chin. There was no way anyone ever did something they were this scared of.

But my body didn't pause. It practically lunged through the door. I wanted to scream. Clench my eyes closed. Throw up. My stomach did its best to run for it. I was falling, falling, falling.

And then I was weightless. The falling sensation was the new normal.

I was flying.

And then I was back in the tent, facing a smiling Louis. I blinked and shook my head.

"You don't need to see the rest." He let go of my hand. He needed better air-conditioning in there. It reeked of vinyl and incense.

"Why not?" I asked, still gathering my thoughts. It had just been getting to the good part.

"It was a memory," he said, sounding contemplative. "My memory. Just a bit of it. It's how I celebrated my nineteenth birthday, though most people called it D-Day."

"It was *real*?" I asked.

"Did you like it?"

Like it? It made the most incredible video game pale in comparison. I stuck my hand out again. "Show me the rest."

He smiled and shook his head. "It gets worse soon after that. I showed you the best part, believe me. It didn't frighten you?"

I shrugged. "Jumping out of the plane was scary, I guess."

His grin widened. "I like you. I think you'd do well."

I cocked my head. "Huh?"

"Would you like to see something else?"

No need to think about that twice. I thrust my hand out.

Louis laughed. "Yes. Hmm. Well. How to put this?" A pause. "Only one freebie per person, I'm afraid."

21

My hand dipped back to my side. "You charge?"

"A man needs to eat."

I dug in my pocket to see what I had left: three quarters and two dimes. Why had I blown it all on fair food? "What can I get for ninety-five cents?"

He gave me a wry grimace. "That would buy you a vision of what I ate for breakfast. It was a very nice omelet. Ham and cheese."

Just my luck. My shoulders slumped. "It's okay."

He snapped his fingers, and I had the sense he might be playing with me. "We could barter!" he said.

"What?"

"We could trade," Louis said. Those pants really needed some suspenders or a better belt. "I give you some memories—or loan them, sometimes—in return for some of your memories. But you're twelve, and I'll need parental consent first."

Why did everything always require your mom or dad saying it was okay? It's not like they were that much more responsible than I was. "Is there a form I need to have them sign?" Maybe they wouldn't read it too carefully.

"What? So you can forge the signature? Nope. I need the parent here personally."

Figured. "So if I bring my parents here, and they say I can, I can sell you some memories, and you'll give me other ones?"

Louis tapped his temple with a finger. "Of course. I've got loads and loads stored up here, some of them dating back to the Middle Ages. You could know what it was like to be a knight of the Round Table. It wasn't round, you know. More of an oval, but King Arthur and the Knights of the Oval Table doesn't sound as good, don't you think?"

"I . . . guess?"

"I've also got some very nice recollections of Babe Ruth in some of his best games. Are you into baseball?"

I shook my head. "My dad might like those." I thought about that scene from World War II again. It had been so vivid. "Do you have anything from the space race? Maybe someone walking on the moon?"

Louis smiled and nodded. "You have a taste for the good stuff, I see. I do happen to have a few of those, captured from some of the astronauts before they passed on. Not the easiest to come by, though, and buying them outright carries an astronomical price tag. Get it? Astronaut? Astronomical?"

When I didn't laugh, he cleared his throat and smoothed his hair back before setting his hat in place. "I can rent you those for a decent rate, though."

I imagined what it would be like to walk on the moon. Low gravity. Seeing the earth hanging above you in the sky. "Why don't you have more people in here?" The tent should have been overflowing. Outside, the muffled throngs headed toward the derby. No one so much as peeked in.

"Video games and movies," Louis said. "People don't believe me. They see the sign, they pass me by."

"So go outside," I said. "Make people see. Once they know what you can do—"

"Let me worry about that, son," he said. I got the feeling he wasn't too concerned with promoting himself. Or maybe he was too weak to really throw himself into the work.

Messing around with memories . . . That could be a useful trick to have with some people. I shifted my feet, trying not to sound too eager or interested. "Could you make someone forget they hate someone else?"

His face grew solemn. More lined. "Your parents aren't going to be fixed by wiping their memories." His voice was soft.

My mouth dropped open. It was too easy to forget what he could do.

"Besides," Louis continued. "You don't want to muck around in people's memories. They don't just disappear, you know. The memories have to go somewhere, unless the person holding them dies. Some memories are better left undisturbed."

"But my parents—"

"You don't steal core memories and emotions. Do you want your parents to change? Become different people? Your memories make you, Benji. Change you. You take those things away, and many people find they're nothing more than a house of cards."

Silence again. Louis stared at me, his face grave. I scowled back. What was the point in having the ability to take memories if you didn't use it? But then again, I hadn't even known this was possible a half hour ago. If Sam hadn't chased me in here . . . I broke the stare with Louis.

"Okay," I said. "And you're here all week?"

"More or less. I might need to wander the grounds now and then, but just wait around if I'm not here. I'll show up eventually."

I liked him, pants up to his armpits and all. He reminded me of my grandfather, back when he was alive. I waved good-bye and left the tent.

CHAPTER

3

SHOUTING

I poked my head out of the tent, nervous Sam might be there. They'd given up, though. The Demolition Derby was starting, and I wandered over to the stadium, my mind lost in thought. Even watching the cars ram into each other in billows of white and gray smoke just reminded me of the scene in the plane, and what it would be like to see more memories.

When my parents found me, I was in the empty stands, scheming about how to come up with more money for memories. Dad had to repeat my name three times before I noticed him.

Mom and Dad were still mad at each other. They didn't

hold hands, and neither of them would look at the other, but they were madder at me. "Are you happy with yourself?" That was the first line Mom tried out on me. And a big chunk of me wanted to shoot back a simple "Yeah." But they were already mad enough without me provoking them.

Also, Kelly was standing behind them, making our "dial it down" gesture—something we used when things were really bad with Mom or Dad. I hung my head. "Sorry," I mumbled, doing my best to sound like it.

"We'll discuss this in the morning," Dad said. "For now, no talking, no video games, no reading."

I checked with Kelly again. She gave a slight nod. Now wasn't the time to make a fuss. Was it a sign of how big of a geek I was when taking away reading privileges was considered a big punishment? I shrugged back. "Okay," I said, but I extended my forefinger twice on my right hand where Kelly was looking: It was the American Sign Language sign for "eleven," meaning we'd talk then. She winked.

The car ride home was dead silent. Kelly played her game, and I was stuck staring out the window at passing cars. Mom and Dad were mutes in the front seat, with no radio to even blunt the silence. My mind was still on the moon, parachutes, and memories. But amid all that tension in the car, I couldn't help but wonder if Louis really knew what he was talking about. Surely *anything* was better than this. If it might make them happier, wasn't it worth the risk of a little changed personality?

Kelly crept into my room right at eleven o'clock. Dad was downstairs watching television. He slept there most nights. The odds of him coming upstairs after the sort of fight he and Mom had had today? Nil. No way Mom would come out of her bedroom, either. Not that Kelly and I could have a humdinger of a party or anything, but as long as we kept our voices down, we were safe.

"What happened tonight?" Kelly asked, perched on the edge of my bed. I had the blinds up, and the full moon outside traced the edge of her face. "What did you do to Sam?"

"Don't worry about that," I said, eager to move on to more interesting subjects. "You'll never guess who I met."

Kelly listened with her mouth half open as I told her about Louis and the memory of parachuting.

"We've been going to the fair since we could walk," Kelly said once I was done. "There's never been any Memory Emporium before."

"He was there today."

"Is this a trick?" She knew I liked to play jokes. I'd once convinced her the school was being taken over by vampires. We'd only been first graders at the time, but she never let me forget it.

"Promise," I said, keeping my gaze steady and my voice calm.

"What's he doing in a place like Livingston?" she asked.

"Searching for someone, I think. A woman with tattoos all over her arms. He asked me about her when I came into the tent. Did you see anyone like that at the fair?"

She shook her head. "I wasn't really looking, though. First Mom and Dad were being such idiots, and then I had to distract them from wanting to kill you. You need to keep your temper better, Benji. It makes things worse."

I stared out the window, watching a passing car wind its way down the road, its headlights illuminating the trees and underbrush on either side of us. We lived five minutes away from the center of town, but with a place as small as Livingston, that meant we lived in the country. "Sorry," I said at last. "I just . . ." I trailed off, unable to finish the sentence.

Kelly nodded. "I know."

I faced her again. "What if we got Louis to take away Mom's and Dad's memories of hating each other? He said it was dangerous, but he's also a thousand years old. Old people are way too cautious."

"Take away their memories?"

"If they could forget they can't stand each other for a minute, maybe they could start forgiving each other, and things would get better."

"Maybe," Kelly said, but she drew the word out, unconvinced.

"We'll go to the fair tomorrow after school and—"

My parents' bedroom door opened and shut, and footsteps came down the hall. Had Mom heard us? Kelly and I froze, staring at each other. Solutions ran through my mind: Kelly could hide in my closet or under my bed. Would Mom check her room first? But the footsteps headed downstairs instead.

Kelly's eyes got wider. We were used to the way our parents fought. There'd be a flare-up, followed by a long period when they didn't talk to each other.

"What is she doing?" I hissed. It felt like my parents were breaking the rules. Like these constant fights were governed by laws, and now Mom was going against all that.

"No idea," Kelly said. "Let's find out."

I didn't want to go out, but Kelly made my mind up for me, taking the lead. And once she was out there, it didn't make sense not to follow her. She did that for me a lot—pushed me to go further than I was comfortable.

We crept out into the landing at the stop of the stairs, crouched low, just in case. Maybe Mom had wanted a drink, or—

They were already talking by the time we could hear anything, and for once, they weren't shouting or even scolding each other. Just a rational discussion. That was more frightening than anything I could remember.

"—over," Mom was saying. "I'm done."

"Whatever," Dad said. "I can call the lawyer in the morning, and we can start getting the paperwork going. Are you sure you don't want the house?"

A pause from Mom. No matter how many times I'd wished they'd get divorced, it hadn't prepared me for this. For the casual way they were talking. Who would get the *house*? This was real. Kelly's face was white in the dim light.

"I'm moving away. Far away," Mom said, then took a breath. "But we still need to decide what to do with the kids."

My stomach plummeted. Dad didn't respond for a while, and when he did, he was frustrated. "We've gone over this fifty times. I'm not changing my mind, so stop nagging about it."

"*Nagging* about it? I'm worried about my children."

Dad's voice got louder. "They're my children, too. Don't you think I worry about them?"

It sped downhill from there. Loud enough that Kelly and I went back to my room. Loud enough that not even my door could drown out the shouting. And they were at it for a solid hour, until Dad's voice was hoarse and Mom stomped up the stairs and slammed the door. But before she did that, Kelly

31

and I had heard what they had settled on, crystal clear.

"It'll be a cold day in Hades before I let you fly off with my kids," Dad had screamed.

Mom came right back with, "And if you think I'm letting you raise them, you're insane."

"Fine," Dad had said.

"See you in court." Mom had then gone into her stomping routine.

Leaving Kelly and me staring at each other.

"It's never been that bad before," Kelly whispered at last.

I nodded, still unsure of what exactly to do or say. *See you in court?* Who actually said that?

"Do you think . . ." I started, then trailed off.

Kelly shook her head. "I don't know what to think. Remember Andrew Caine's parents? That divorce lasted almost a year, and he was a wreck the whole time. If Mom and Dad get mad enough, this could get bad."

My stomach felt like it wanted to drop to China. "How bad?"

My sister thought for a moment. "Maybe the courts decide to get all even-steven—they split us up. You go with Dad, I go with Mom. I don't know." She sounded close to tears.

It was a long time before either of us fell asleep.

CHAPTER

4

GENEVIEVE

Kelly and I planned it on the bus ride the next morning: walk to the fair after school and see if we could persuade Louis to monkey around with our parents' memories. Maybe if they forgot they hated each other, we could avoid this whole mess.

"Do you think it'll work?" I asked.

Kelly shrugged. "Not sure."

Trees and telephone poles streaked by outside the window. "We could talk to them," I said at last. "Before we try this, I mean."

Kelly only grunted. I couldn't blame her. It felt like if we talked about this too much, it might take us to a place we didn't want to go.

School was a haze. I ate my lunch when I was supposed to but didn't taste any of it. Other kids laughed or joked around, and Kelly and I pretended to laugh with them. But we shared quick glances that said we were thinking about other things.

Sam Hyde was there, of course. And he was still glaring at me. I didn't care.

The bell rang at last, and I met Kelly in front of the school and headed down the road. I'd called Dad earlier in the day, telling him Kelly had lost one of her games at the fair. It had been her idea. I was already in enough trouble with my parents as it was. Dad wasn't happy, but he'd agreed to let us go try to find it and pick us up later. It was nice to be outside under a clear blue sky, our backpacks slung over our shoulders. We still weren't speaking, but we were finally *doing* something. Fixing things.

"Do you think it hurts to sell a memory?" Kelly asked.

I kicked a stone the size of a golf ball, and it went skittering down the road for ten feet before hitting a rut and careening into the underbrush. "It didn't hurt when Louis let me see D-Day. I figure he just . . . takes the memories. And once they're gone, you can't even know you're missing them, right? You don't remember them."

The air was crisp, and people in town were out mowing

their lawns or heading to the grocery store. The leaves had started to change, with individual trees bursting out in red or orange or yellow while the rest of them waited another week or two. That's when the huge tour buses would roll in, bringing people who rode for hours just to look at some leaves. The leaves were pretty and all, but didn't everybody have trees of their own? Maine couldn't be the only place in the world that experienced autumn.

Kelly thought about it. "Maybe." She still didn't sound convinced that Louis was for real. I'd tried to persuade her, but she was mainly just going along with me on this because she had no better ideas about what to do.

I swallowed. "They might not have meant it."

"They meant it," Kelly said.

"But maybe we could—"

"They meant it."

We took a left on High Street to go to the fairgrounds. The rumble of rides and the announcer's droning voice at the animal competitions echoed down the road, even from this far away. Maine county fairs were the same every year. Tractor pulls, horse races, Demolition Derbies. I could smell the doughnuts already. Not that I wanted any right now.

"We'll go in," Kelly said. "Go straight to Louis and tell him our problem. No talking about seeing memories. No distractions. Right?"

I nodded. This could work.

We had to pay to get in, of course, and there was a line already—other families mostly, though not as many as yesterday. Kelly and I each plopped five dollars down and made a beeline for The Memory Emporium. What if Louis was gone? What if our only idea for fixing our parents turned out to be—

There it was. Purple, green, and white stripes, with the sign still out front. I breathed a sigh of relief, then froze. Something like a big sticky note had been added to the sign. We walked up to the tent to get a better look.

Out for Lunch. Be Back Soon. —Louis

"Great," I said. My shoulders slumped.

Kelly smiled. "The tent's here, just like you said. He'll be back any minute." We stood off to the side, watching the crowd for any sign of Louis. My feet were fidgety. What if Louis didn't want to go along with our plan?

"Do you notice something?" Kelly asked.

I raised my eyebrows. "Huh?"

"Something is . . . off. With the people. They look confused. Or lost."

And once she mentioned it, I could see it, too. Not all of them, but quite a few. People would be walking by and suddenly stop and stare around, like they'd forgotten why they'd come that way. And while the fair could be a confusing place, some of the people manning the booths were doing it, too. No—all of them were.

A Boy Scout leader stared at me, pamphlets advertising Scouting clutched in his fist, his jaw slack and a tiny trail of drool leaking out of one corner of his mouth. I glanced behind me, hoping he was focused on something else, but nothing was there. When I looked back, he was wiping his face and frowning in confusion at the crumpled mess of pamphlets in his hands.

A knot formed in my stomach. I licked my lips. "You don't think Louis would have done this, do you?"

"You're the one who met him. *Something* is off with these people, though. Maybe he's connected."

"But Louis helped me yesterday. He didn't—"

A woman approached the tent. I grabbed my sister by the elbow and dragged her to a neighboring booth where they were hawking leather hats.

"What?" she asked.

I nodded at the woman, who had stopped in front of The Memory Emporium to inspect it. She looked like a college student. Pretty and tall, with one of those boy haircuts. Dark hair. Dressed in jeans and a T-shirt despite the chill in the air. Her arms were completely covered in tattoos, right down to her wrists, where the tattoos ended abruptly, making it look like she had a long-sleeved shirt on. The tattoos themselves were hard to distinguish. One minute I thought I saw a man screaming in agony, but then it looked more like a bloody knife. It wasn't that the tattoos were magically changing. It was just that they were more an abstract work of art instead of hearts with "Mom" written on them.

None of the images were pleasant.

She took the note down and walked into the tent.

Kelly stared at me. "Who was that?" she asked.

I shook my head. "Louis warned me about her yesterday. He was looking for her, and he said if I saw her, I should come get him."

"Maybe she's his assistant?" Kelly offered. "Or granddaughter?"

Louis didn't seem like the kind of old man who'd hire a woman like that. Granddaughter was possible, I supposed. You didn't get to pick your family. "Let's wait for him."

Kelly smirked at me. "Afraid to talk to a girl?"

"No, but . . . did you see her tattoos?"

My sister pulled me forward. "We came here to see if we could help our parents. You can't let some tattoos get in the way of that, Benji."

I wasn't scared of the tattoos. Creeped out, yes. But I was mainly worried because Louis had warned me about her. But maybe my eyes had been playing tricks on me, or maybe Louis was actually in the tent and had just forgotten to take the note down. I let Kelly lead me inside. We were in Livingston, Maine. Nothing bad could happen here. Right?

The woman was sitting in Louis's chair behind the table, staring at the tent's flap door when we entered. For a moment, she was backlit, as if the light didn't want to fall on her. The way she sat in that chair made it look like a throne. All she was missing was a pedestal and some cowering servants.

And then the moment was gone, and she was just a woman in a chair. "Yes?" she asked. Her voice was low, and an image of a deep lake flashed through my mind when I heard it. Glacial.

Kelly and I struggled to speak, neither of us finding our voices. The woman stared at Kelly for a moment, and *something* happened. I wasn't sure what. One minute, my sister was full of determination and resolve, and the next, the edge had left her. She seemed more relaxed. Calm.

The woman turned her gaze to me, and a sharp pain blossomed behind my right eye, as if someone had heated a needle until it was glowing red, then shoved it into my brain. I shouted in surprise and agony, but it vanished. "You've been talking to Louis, I see," the woman said.

I massaged my eye and managed to get out, "Where is he?" And what had that pain been?

She gave a small smile. "He's tired and asked me to run things for a while."

"Are you his granddaughter?" Kelly asked.

Her smile widened. "How did you guess? My name's Genevieve."

She didn't look anything like Louis. Then again, who knew what he'd looked like when he was younger?

"What can I help you with?" she asked.

"Nothing," I said. "We just wanted to talk to him." She kept staring at me, not saying a word. "We can come back later," I added. Now it was my turn to grab Kelly and try dragging her out.

Kelly wrenched her arm out of my grasp. "Can you do it, too?"

"Do what?" Genevieve asked.

"Give memories," Kelly said. "Buy them. Loan them. That sort of thing." She was worried about *seeing memories*? Five minutes ago, our only concern had been to fix our parents. We didn't have time to waste on looking at memories.

"She's just his assistant, Kelly," I told him. "We can come—"

"It isn't hard," Genevieve said, giving a slight shrug. "Is there a particular memory you're interested in seeing?"

Kelly nodded. "Something from the Wild West. I want to see the gunfight at the OK Corral, or Butch Cassidy. Do you have anything like that?" She'd inherited Dad's love of Westerns, but this was ridiculous. What happened to "no distractions"? Why was she ignoring me?

The smile returned to Genevieve's face. "You've thought this through, I see. That's wonderful. I happen to have something I think you'd just adore. The memory of the man who assassinated Wild Bill Hickok. Would that do?"

Kelly smiled back. "That'd be awesome."

"Good," Genevieve said. "But it'll cost you."

Kelly's face clouded over in confusion. "Don't I get my first memory free? That's what—"

"Has he been doing that again?" Genevieve tsked. "He's never going to keep the business up if he does that. I keep telling him, but he never listens. I could show you something minor, I suppose. A bystander at the *Hindenburg* crash? Just to give you a taste. You have to pay for the good stuff."

"Show me the *Hinderburg* thing, then," Kelly said, reaching out her hand. "Prove it."

"Kelly," I started, but she ignored me and clasped Genevieve's hand. My sister's body went stiff. I hadn't seen what I looked like yesterday when Louis showed me World War II. Her eyes rolled into the back of her head, and her whole body shook, as if she were in the middle of a violent earthquake. Genevieve held on tight to her hand.

I wanted to reach out and stop it, but I didn't know if it would have bad results. Maybe it would leave my sister comatose. Was the woman really just showing Kelly the *Hindenburg*?

What was that, anyway? Maybe she was stealing Kelly's memories, draining her of everything she had. Thinking about the change that had come over Kelly when she looked at Genevieve, my knees went weak, and I had to lean against the table.

Maybe Genevieve had already stolen some of Kelly's memories.

The shaking got worse. Kelly's mouth opened and shut in convulsions. Her eyes were totally white, and her right arm twitched nonstop. Her breath came in quick gasps that sounded far too shallow. Was she choking?

Genevieve's eyes were closed, and she was smiling slightly. She took a deep breath through her nose, as if relishing a scent or a feeling. This wasn't right. She might be draining every memory Kelly had. I pictured my sister left like she was now, forever. Helpless. Unconscious. Why had we come here? Why had I let her take Genevieve's hand? I stopped worrying about hurting Kelly: If I did nothing, she might die in front of me while I—

The shaking stopped. My sister opened her eyes, a big smile plastered across her face. Her eyes went straight to mine. "Benji, you should have seen it. It was this huge blimp, and it exploded. I've never *seen* a fireball that big—not even in the movies. And this was in person. I was right there." The smile became more hesitant. Less certain. "There were screams . . ."

"Well," Genevieve said, her voice bright and cheery. "Is

that proof enough? Who's ready for something even more impressive?"

Kelly nodded immediately.

I cleared my throat. "We can't afford it."

Genevieve flicked her fingers at the air, as if she were shooing away a pesky fly. "Costs? Who said anything about costs? This is barter, baby. Memories for memories. I'm sure we can reach an agreement."

Kelly tried to answer, but I cut her off. "We don't have the parental permission forms signed yet."

"You're both mature enough, aren't you?" Genevieve asked. "I don't see any need for some pesky old forms. We're young, right? We don't believe in such things."

Kelly started. "We'd love—"

"To think about it," I finished. "Can we have some time? What memories are you buying, anyway?"

"Anything you're selling," Genevieve answered. Her eyes were bright and alive, even in the darkened light of the tent. They made me want to study them closer, see them better. But when I stared too long, the pain returned behind my eye, hotter and fiercer than ever. I broke the gaze.

She continued as if nothing had happened, though maybe there was a slight tightness at the edge of her mouth. Frustration? "Say your parents forced you to take piano lessons for five years. I could take five years of piano practice off your hands and pay you top dollar. Then someone who wants to be able to play the piano but doesn't feel like practicing for years to get good . . . I can sell those memories to them. For a bit more than I paid, but everyone's happy. Nothing sinister about it, young man."

Her low voice sounded earnest but confused, as if she couldn't understand how anyone would have thought differently.

"Right," Kelly said. "See, Benji? Nothing sinister."

Why was Kelly so eager to do this? We hadn't come to see memories today. We'd come to get help for our parents. And if there was nothing sinister, why did I feel so creeped out? Why did her tattoos show images of people being tortured one moment, their skin sliced open, and then suddenly an image of a house burning to the ground? Again, you couldn't watch the tattoos physically change shape. It was more like cloud gazing, thinking one looked like a dog at first, only to have it change into an ice cream cone the next time you checked.

Just way more evil.

Genevieve tried again. "It doesn't have to be piano, of course. You'd be surprised what else people will pay for. Maybe embarrassing moments. Ever been made to look like an idiot in front of your friends? Had someone beat you in a fight? You don't need to remember those things, do you?"

"Why would someone pay for things like that?" Kelly asked, still curious.

"Sometimes it's best not to ask questions, especially if you don't want to know the answers," Genevieve said. "Do we have a deal?"

Kelly wanted to say yes. I could see it in her eyes, the way they got wider when she was eager. But she looked at me first, and I shook my head. She chewed the inside of her bottom lip. "Can we think it over some?" Kelly asked at last.

I breathed a sigh of relief.

Genevieve gave a slight shrug. "Naturally. Come back any time you want, but I have to get them before the end of the week. I've made arrangements for a group of buyers to meet me on Friday, and they're a very . . . impatient group."

"When is Louis coming back?" I asked.

"Like I said, he's been overexerting himself. I talked him into taking a break."

I hoped he was okay. The thought of Genevieve doing something to him was upsetting, but very believable. "Then we'll think about it," I said. "Right now, we've got to be going. Our parents are going to be wondering where we are."

I dragged Kelly out of the tent without letting her say another word.

CHAPTER

5

HOLES

"What's the big deal?" Kelly asked. "It was rude of us to just run."

"We didn't 'just run,'" I answered, leading her back to the exhibit hall. Somewhere far away from Genevieve. Out in the fresh air, I wondered at my feelings just moments ago. This was the Livingston Fair. People were wandering around, eating fries or doughnuts, browsing fudge and T-shirts. There was nothing wicked at work here, was there?

When I'd been with Louis, I'd felt positive and upbeat. But when we'd been with Genevieve, I'd felt like I was about to be murdered and left in a dark alley.

We got to the hall and took a seat by the pumpkin competition. Enormous misshapen pumpkins lay bloated on the floor. "What happened back there?" I asked.

Kelly raised her eyebrows. "You mean besides you chickening out of doing what we came here for?"

I shook my head. "I didn't chicken out. We didn't come here to see memories. We came to help our parents and we never even came close to talking about them."

Kelly sighed. "What in the world would we need to help our parents with? You think there's something we could do to make them fight less?"

No doubt about it. Genevieve had done something to my sister. "No," I said. "But I think we could get them to stop thinking about divorcing and each taking one of us."

I'd said that last bit too loudly. The other people in the hall stopped what they were doing and stared at us. I felt like I was under a microscope.

Kelly's face had paled. "What?"

"Don't you remember? Last night?"

"Nothing happened last night," Kelly said, her forehead crinkled in confusion. "We came home. We went to bed."

"No. You came to talk to me, and they had a huge fight."

I told her more about it, but it was clear Kelly had none of those memories. And she could tell I was being serious. She knew something had happened to her, and she wasn't happy about it. She wouldn't meet my eyes, and she was chewing on her bottom lip enough to put a hole through it.

"We need to get my memories back," she said at last, trying to stand up and leave.

I grabbed her arm and kept her sitting. "You don't get it," I said. "All she had to do was look at you, and you changed. I think she can steal thoughts with a glance. Yesterday, when Sam and I ran into Louis's tent, the old guy knew our names, what we were fighting about—everything. He even knew about Mom and Dad, and all he'd needed to do was look me in the eye. She can probably do the same thing. We can't go back there, Kelly."

But it didn't matter what I said. When Dad picked us up at five, Kelly was still upset, leaving me to tell Dad that we hadn't found the game after all, in an attempt to explain her mood. The whole car ride home, she kept putting a hand to her head, as if she'd be able to tell something had been taken from her. She didn't speak during dinner, and she went straight to her room as soon as her plate was clean.

Mom and Dad were too busy being angry to notice. They were still mad at me from my stunt yesterday, so I was stuck doing all the chores around the house. Empty the trash. Do the dishes. Clean the bathroom. Break down the boxes in the garage. Why weren't they making Kelly do it for losing her imaginary game? Maybe they thought losing the game was punishment enough. Who knew? Between the two of them, Mom and Dad kept me hopping the whole evening, and I was exhausted when they finally decided I'd had enough.

I trudged up the stairs at nine, pausing to knock at Kelly's door.

She didn't answer.

I debated knocking again but eventually decided against it. She'd had a long day, she was still upset, and I had a mound of homework to be done before bed.

We'd worry about fixing things in the morning.

A half hour later, Kelly slipped into my room. She was fully dressed—coat and shoes on, ready to go. I frowned at her. "What are you doing?"

Her chin was squared in determination. "I'm going back. Tonight. Now."

I got up from my desk. "That's a terrible idea, Kelly. You can't be this impulsive. Remember what I told you? If we—"

"You're too scared, Benji. You always are. I'm not going to get my memories back by just worrying about them. That witch stole them from me, and I'm going to make her undo it. Now, are you coming with me or not?"

I put my hands on her shoulders, staring her right in the face. "I know I'm hesitant. And usually you're right. I should be more assertive. But not this time, Kelly. You don't know what you're talking about. Can't you just believe me for once?"

She stared back. I'd known this had upset her, but I hadn't really known how deeply. Kelly was always the rock. Hotheaded. Confident. To see a tremble at the corner of her mouth, a tightness around her lips . . . she was scared, and that terrified me.

For a moment, I thought my plea wasn't going to be enough. But her shoulders slumped. Did I catch a hint of disappointment in her expression?

"You're right, Benji." She shook her head. "I don't know what I was thinking."

Thank goodness. "We can go find Louis," I told her. She needed to have a plan—to feel like she was working toward a solution. "He'll be able to fix this. We'll go together. Tomorrow."

She gave me a final nod. We hugged, and she went back to her room.

Crisis averted.

I slogged through my algebra homework and most of history, but I was too distracted. My mind kept churning over our predicament. Finally, I gave up on homework and went to sleep. My dreams were filled with swirling tattoos and the constant feeling of falling. I woke up in the middle of the night, breathless and sweating. In my nightmare, Genevieve had been cutting into Kelly's head with a scalpel, picking at her brain and laughing while my sister lay on her bed, screaming. I was forced to watch, tied to a steel chair with razor wire around my arms and legs. The more I tried to get free to help Kelly, the deeper the razors cut into my skin, but I kept struggling until bone was showing through the slices.

It was a rough night.

My alarm went off at 6:25. I dragged myself out of bed and to the bathroom, which for once wasn't occupied by Kelly. One shower later, I was feeling much better about life. I did a lot of my best thinking in the shower. Everything seemed simpler there. Kelly and I would go back to the fair, but we'd avoid Genevieve. She couldn't steal memories from us if she couldn't see us. We'd find Louis, tell him about our problems, and he'd fix them. I came out of the bathroom dressed and ready for the day, fully expecting to find Kelly there waiting for me impatiently. Neither of us ever used Mom and Dad's bathroom.

No sign of her.

She must have already been downstairs eating breakfast. If my sleep had been bad, hers must have been worse. She was the one whose memories Genevieve had stolen, after all. So I plodded down to the kitchen.

No bowl out for cereal. No Kelly reading a book at the table.

She'd overslept. That had to be it.

I rushed back upstairs to Kelly's door. It was closed, and

the picture of the Tenth Doctor stared back at me disapprovingly. I knocked, softly at first.

"Kelly?" Something was wrong. I'd known it since I'd gotten up, but I didn't want to face it. As long as I just knocked softly, it could mean she was still asleep.

"Kelly?" I repeated, knocking louder. No answer.

I opened the door.

Her bed hadn't been slept in. Her backpack sat by her desk, all the books inside it. The window was open, and a draft sent her red curtains into billows.

It clicked: she'd gone back to Genevieve.

I didn't want to believe it, but it's what I would have done if I were her, and in many ways, I practically was. We were twins. I'd been friends with her since I first came into the world. She'd gone to confront Genevieve, and that had been a huge mistake. I should have been more forceful last night. Kelly wouldn't have let me leave her sight if she'd been in my position. And now it was too late.

My dream from last night flashed through my head, and I tried to shove it away. Kelly would be okay. She had to be.

Breakfast was a blur. I shoveled food into my mouth quickly and efficiently, then stuffed a bagel and a can of soda into my bag for later. I thought up any number of excuses to give Mom when she came home from her morning jog and wondered where Kelly was. Dad was already at work. It didn't matter. Mom was still gone by the time the bus came.

I did my best to stay out of panic mode. Kelly had gone to Genevieve, but the woman wouldn't have done anything really bad. This was Livingston.

My sister had to be fine. I'd cut class to go over to the fair and search for her. I should probably go to my parents, but I didn't want Kelly to get into trouble for running off. As long as this was just about my sister making a bad choice and getting in trouble, then it wasn't about something bigger. Kidnapping or worse.

All my plans flew out the window when I got to school and caught a glimpse of Kelly's dark hair bobbing its way into school, and a wave of relief washed over me.

It took some running, but I caught up to her just as she was getting to her locker. We had five minutes before the homeroom bell rang.

"Kelly!" I shouted out, never more grateful to see her.

She glanced up from her locker, then looked back down, her expression blank.

A pit of worry sprang up in my stomach. "Kelly?"

She messed up her combination and sighed. "Who are you, and what do you want?"

"Very funny. Where have you been? I was worried sick."

"Look, kid," she said. "I'm going to be late for class. I don't have time for some dork to play tricks on me."

I frowned at her. "Kelly, it's me. Benji?"

She got her locker open and started taking out books. "Great. You know your name. I'm happy for you, kid." She closed the door to her locker and headed to homeroom, which was right by us.

I followed her.

"Where did you go last night?" I asked, still hoping that somehow this was some big misunderstanding. Could she have amnesia?

"What is this, twenty questions? Get. Lost."

But, of course, I couldn't get lost; I sat next to her in homeroom. Kelly ignored me, despite the anxious tone to my voice. Mrs. Hutchins had to ask me to stop talking twice, and some of the other kids in class gave my sister and me strange looks, no doubt wondering what the twins were up to.

Things didn't get any better during Earth Science. Kelly walked in and waved cheerily to Sam Hyde, who nodded back at her like they'd been best friends forever.

I was floored. It was like I'd fallen into a strange alternate reality with all the same people, but none of them behaved the same.

"You went back to her, didn't you?" I asked Kelly as soon as class started.

She looked at me out of the corner of her eye, then sighed

and turned to face me straight on—Mr. Van Houten was focused on writing on the board for the moment. "Listen, kid," Kelly said. "I don't know who you are, and I don't know what you're talking about, but if you get me in trouble with Van Houten, I'm going to knock your teeth in. So shut up and leave me alone." And then she rolled her eyes at Sam, who laughed and smirked.

I sat there, stunned. Knock my teeth in? It was one thing to have some of the bullies at school say stupid things. That's what bullies did. But to have my best friend—my *twin*—threaten me like that?

She had to be joking. Even if Genevieve had taken some of her memories, she couldn't have changed her personality. I forced a small laugh, trying to show I was in on it. Maybe she'd drop it then, and we could go back to normal.

But she didn't drop it. Not during Mr. Van Houten's class. Not at lunch. Not at all. I sat alone in the cafeteria, watching as my twin went up to some of the football players and cheerleaders and somehow managed to talk her way into sitting at their table. Sam Hyde put his arm around her, like she was his girlfriend. Some of the other guys and girls at the table gave them odd looks, but they went along with it.

Genevieve had caused this. I didn't know how, and I wasn't sure why, but she'd done it. She'd taken the memories of me from my sister, and she'd given Kelly different ones in return. Genevieve must have gotten to Sam, too.

But why?

I couldn't stand it anymore. Kelly had to have *some* memory of me left in her. If I could just confront her and get her to remember, this could all be fixed. I'd convinced her yesterday. I could do it again.

Taking a deep breath, I got up from my table and walked across the room. My stomach felt like it was trying to drop out through my feet, and I actually stumbled once, even over the smooth cafeteria floor. One of the group members noticed me coming and elbowed the guy next to him. Before long, they were all watching me approach. All but Kelly.

The moisture had vanished from my mouth, and I balled one hand into a fist, just to keep my nerve. "What happened?" I asked her, ignoring the others.

She didn't turn around.

"Kelly," I said.

That got her attention. She turned and frowned at me, her mouth full of baloney sandwich. Her favorite. "What?"

"Why did you go back to Genevieve?"

She sighed and looked at the rest of the table. "Can you believe this kid?" Kelly said. "He's been bugging me the whole day. Pretending we're friends."

"Friends?" I said. "We're twins! You're my sister!"

"See?" Kelly said.

Sam took another bite of his turkey sandwich. "Delusional."

Matt and Michael exchanged confused glances. *They* knew Kelly and I were twins. But they decided to go along with it. "You want us to get rid of him?" Matt asked, half standing up.

Kelly shrugged. "If he keeps going, I guess. But I'm betting he'll leave on his own."

She was betting right. I turned around and ran out of the room, fighting back tears. We weren't allowed to leave the cafeteria without a pass, but the room monitor had some idea of what was going on. She didn't stop me.

I hurried outside and sat on a bench, sucking in fresh air and trying to convince myself this wasn't happening. When I'd first met Louis—when he'd shown me that airplane scene—I'd been so excited.

If I'd only known.

I should never have told Kelly about it. Never gone to talk to Genevieve. I should have just ignored the lousy tent like everyone else at the fair. They obviously knew better. I was an idiot.

The tears had stopped trying to leak out the edges of my eyes. At least I knew what was causing this.

Something had to be done.

I'd go to Genevieve and convince her to give the memories

back. Maybe she didn't realize what she'd done. Maybe it was an accident. Maybe I could trade some of my memories for Kelly's really important ones.

The rest of the school day was a chore. I kept my head down, answered questions only when asked, and tried to ignore the rest of the kids. Word was out that something was up between Kelly and me, and several students came up to me to ask what had happened. I brushed them all off.

When the final bell rang, I hurried out past the buses, wanting to go fast to make sure I didn't see Kelly. Her last class was on the second floor, on the far end of the school.

The sky had clouded over, and the temperature was dropping fast. It might snow tonight—not an unheard of thing for September in Maine. I hadn't brought my thick coat, not expecting to be outside for long. I wrapped my windbreaker around me as tight as I could and walked quickly to stay warm. The wind whipped through the trees, tearing leaves down from the branches.

Hardly anyone else was out. They raced through their errands and rushed home to start a fire in the woodstove or put some hot chocolate on the burner. It was the kind of afternoon that promised a long winter full of snowy nights without electricity. The kind of afternoon you wanted to spend with your family or a good book.

Family. Better not think about that. Did Kelly remember

where she lived? What would she say when (if) she got home and saw pictures of me all over the place? Maybe she'd start believing me then.

I got to the fair, and its attendance was low, too. After the entrance fee, I was down to $3.72. That wasn't going to help persuade Genevieve very much. If I couldn't find Louis, I'd have to count on appealing to her sense of pity.

If she had any.

I wandered the fair looking for signs of Louis, but my heart wasn't in it. I knew Genevieve had caused this. She could fix it. Trying to find the old man just seemed to be delaying helping Kelly, and I wanted to help her this instant.

The rest of the fair looked suspicious. Sinister. I caught several people giving me dark glances. The "Jesus Saves" booth was shuttered early. The fudge lady had gone home. The people left at the fair were dressed in leather and grouped in clusters, laughing loudly and tossing cigarette butts over their shoulders. The ones who weren't doing that were just staring off into space, not making eye contact with anyone else. Creeped out, I made a beeline for the tent, then froze.

It was gone, replaced by a full-fledged fair trailer. A nice one, with steps leading up to it, curtains in the windows, and bloodred paint. The sign over the door read:

MADAME G'S HOUSE OF WONDERS
MEMORIES, FORTUNES, MAGIC, AND MORE

The trailer had a line that stretched out into the next stall, even with the fair being practically empty. This was not good. If Genevieve had messed up Kelly that easily, what could she do on a bigger scale?

I got in line, paying close attention to people as they walked in and comparing them to the same people when they walked out. Were they different? Meaner? Maybe I was imagining it. Everyone chattered excitedly on the way in, and once they were through, they all seemed pleased enough. That was how the trailer was getting so much attention so quickly. The people around me in line talked about how awesome they'd heard this was. How Madame G could make you remember things you'd forgotten, or never experienced before to begin with. Some of the crowd passed it off as parlor tricks, but they were still in line, waiting just like me.

It took forever before it was my turn. As I waited, I noticed a man make several trips with a wheelbarrow, transporting dirt and rocks from somewhere behind the trailer to somewhere off in another corner of the fairgrounds. "Digging a tunnel to China?" I asked him as he walked by me the third time.

He set the wheelbarrow down, cocked his head to the side, and stared at me long enough for me to feel uncomfortable. He was looking *through* me, making me feel like I was talking to one of those animatronic robots at Disney World. His hands were caked with dirt, and a few of his fingernails had split. I spotted several oozing blisters that made me want to cringe. He shook his head. "I can't remember." And continued on with his load.

I was going to talk to him again when he came back, but it was my turn at last.

The trailer's door was mahogany. The red walls were carved from wood as well, a series of fantastical scenes. Men sprouting wings and flying. Centaurs on the hunt. Demons leading young women off into the forest. I entered and the door shut behind me.

At least fifty candles lit the room. Curtains lined every wall, making it seem like we were still in a tent. There were windows, but they were all covered.

Genevieve sat at a round table with a crystal ball on it. She had a long flowing dress on—one that covered her tattoos completely. She'd draped a chain around her short brown hair, leaving a small blue crystal in the middle of her forehead. She smiled when she saw me.

"Back again, Benji?"

I strode over to her and did my best to loom. "What did

you do to my sister?"

She laughed. "Nothing she wasn't paid for, I assure you. Kelly came to me late last night. She had some grandiose ideas about confronting me to get back the memories that she sold, but after some calm conversation, she and I worked out a trade both of us found fair. Why? Does she have some complaints?"

"She doesn't remember me anymore!"

The smile stayed on her face, and she shrugged. "Of course she doesn't. True friendship fetches an enormous sum on the Memoria Mensarius these days. That's the black market for memories. So many depressed people. So much loneliness. She came to me last night, troubled about her life. I fixed all that, and even threw in a cute boyfriend. True, I had to monkey with his memories too, but I like to go above and beyond the call of duty for my clients."

I shook my head. "No. Kelly wouldn't have sold her memories of me away."

"Don't be such a Boy Scout." Genevieve sighed. "Everyone has a price. The key is finding out what it is, and being willing to pay it."

"You tricked her. The Kelly I know would have rather died than turn into the Kelly I saw today."

Genevieve examined her fingernails, glancing up at me.

"Kids like you always see things in black and white. Right and wrong. Eventually, you find out it's a lot more complicated than that. You see that . . ." She trailed off in thought.

I narrowed my eyes and clenched my fist tighter. "You're not that much older than me."

She came back to herself in a flash, eyes narrowing. "It's not the age that counts. It's the mileage. Do you know what I've had to go through? What I—" She took a deep breath and continued in a calmer voice. "Your sister betrayed you? So what? Do you think you're the first that's happened to? At least she got something in return. Memories are like a good garden. They need to be pruned regularly, and the fruit needs to be harvested. Kelly still has friends. She'll be great."

She gave me a sly smile and tilted her head down to look at me through her eyelashes. "You miss her so much? Forget her. You'll feel fine, and I can give you something remarkable in return."

I stared at her, and for an instant, I considered it. The hurt of the day was still too raw. By the next second, I was ashamed I'd even thought about it. I turned from Genevieve and dashed out of the trailer. She didn't follow me.

I ran until the line that stretched out in front of her trailer was nothing more than a memory. And even then, I wanted to keep going. To race right back to yesterday and stop Kelly from returning to her.

But I knew there was no way I could run that far. I had to do something to fix this, and I had to do it fast.

If only I knew what.

6

EMPTY BOTTLES

Out in the fresh air, away from Genevieve's influence, a plan became obvious as soon as I thought about it: find Louis. When I'd first met him, he'd been looking for Genevieve. Now he was my only hope for getting Kelly back to normal. Genevieve had mentioned being able to sell the memories on the black market. Memoria Mensarius? There had to be some way to take them out of her mind and give them to someone else, just like Louis had shown me World War II, but permanently.

Louis was the key.

But where was he?

He'd said he wasn't going to leave the fair. Now that Genevieve had taken down his tent and replaced it with her trailer, I suspected Louis had been pushed out. Maybe she'd locked him up somewhere. Or drugged him. Could you steal sleep and force it on someone? If you could steal friendship and love, why not?

Where would he be? He didn't have a house in town. A place as small as Livingston couldn't hide a zany old man like that. He had to be on the fairgrounds somewhere.

Back behind the livestock pens, over on the opposite side of the stadium, sat the RV section, where the people who worked at the fair stayed each night. They traveled around the countryside from fair to fair, running the different rides, selling their food or wares. No one ever went there. There was nothing to see.

But it made sense that Louis had a trailer of his own, and maybe that was where he was now. I could find him, ask him to steal the memories back, and then everything would be fixed.

I got to the trailers and stopped. Staring. There were tons of them: white, beaten down, arranged in haphazard rows. It would take forever to search them all. It was already after four o'clock. If Mom was home, she'd be worrying about where I was, if Kelly hadn't already shown up to totally freak her out.

One problem at a time. My parents had gotten over it when I ran off at the fair the other day. They hadn't caught on about yesterday's fib. What was one more tiny lie?

I started walking up and down the trailers, trying to look into each one without appearing too nosy. But I was just too short. I couldn't peer into the windows and see what was inside. And even if I could, a lot of them had their shades drawn. It made sense—in a place with everyone so tightly packed together, you'd want some privacy.

Going down one of the rows, I heard footsteps from behind me. I turned, but no one was there. My heart started beating heavily, and my breath sped up. I had to stay calm. No use letting my imagination make things worse. But when I started walking again, I heard the footsteps once more. Big thudding ones that had to come from someone large. Threatening.

Coming my way.

Imagination or not, I didn't want to meet whoever this was. I darted underneath the trailer next to me, rolling through the grass to get away. It was cramped and smelled of motor oil, and I scraped my arm against something sharp, but I kept rolling until I was out on the other side, away from whoever had been after me.

I sat there a moment, looking at my dirty jeans and arms and trying not to feel too much like an idiot. I was bleeding from the scrape, and for what? Because I'd been worried someone was after me? *Ridiculous.*

But still, when I started walking again, I was careful to step lightly and do my best to make as little noise as possible. Just in case.

I started to hurry, then reminded myself to slow down. I had to not look suspicious. I was just here, going over to . . . a friend's trailer. Yeah. Just visiting a friend at the fair. Nothing suspicious at all. I turned a corner to go down another row of trailers that looked the same as the one I'd just come from. I kept my pace steady and tried to look at different trailers by just moving my eyes—not my head.

Things went fine for a minute or two, but the footsteps came back soon after. And even though I knew a suspicious person would do it, I hurried anyway, taking a turn without really looking where it took me. In my rush, I'd gone down the back side of a row of trailers. There were cables and hoses to walk over and navigate, as well as a patch of mud that threatened to go over the tops of my shoes. No matter how much I tried to be quiet, my feet squelched with every step. But the footsteps were gone. Had I escaped them again?

I edged to the end of the row, hoping to peer around the corner and see if someone was there. It had to be some misunderstanding. Maybe a fair worker was busy on some chore around here. The second I peeked out, an enormous hand flashed around and clamped on my neck, dragging me out into the open as I squawked in surprise and fear.

The hand pushed me upright. "What are you doing?" a voice asked. A big burly man in overalls loomed over me, frowning down at me. He had a bushy beard and intense eyes. Not vacant like some of the other people I'd seen. He was focused. Alert. Suspicious.

I froze. "Um. Nothing. Just . . . looking for my grand-father's trailer." I took another step and slipped. I had to windmill my arms to stay upright, but even that wasn't going to do it. I was going to fall face-first into all that muck.

And then the bearded man caught my hand and steadied me. He smiled. "You'll never find him back here. What's his name?"

I blinked. I didn't know Louis's last name. What kind of grandkid didn't know that? "Pop Pop," I said, trying to keep my voice steady and confident and hoping for once I appeared younger than I was.

The guy chuckled.

Before he could ask more questions, I added, "He's famous. You must have heard of him. He runs The Memory Emporium?"

"Ah," he said. "That . . . guy. He's over on the other end of the trailers. I'll show you."

He wasn't going to take no for an answer. As nice as he was being, he was also no doubt suspicious of me and wanted to check out my story. Fair enough. I just hoped Louis played along when he saw me.

The man guided me back to firm ground and through the rows of trailers until he pointed at one. "That's his. Let's see if he's in."

He strode to the door and rapped on it.

Nothing. He knocked again.

Part of me wanted Louis to not be home. Then I could just pretend to be disappointed, and the bearded man could let me go. But that would only solve my immediate problem. If Louis wasn't there, then I had no idea what to do about Genevieve and Kelly.

Another knock.

Still nothing.

"Doesn't look like he's here," the man said. "Why don't you go play in the real fair? Most people don't take kindly—"

The trailer door opened to show Louis standing in a worn velvet robe. He was blinking and rubbing his milky eyes, clearly having just gotten up. "What's going on?"

"Pop Pop!" I rushed forward to give him a hug.

He *oofed* in surprise. Was he going to understand what I was trying to do? Would he object? I'd barely even talked to him the other day. Why did I trust him so much? After a moment, he patted me on the back. "I missed you, boy. Won't you come in?"

He'd gone along with it. Thank goodness. We both waved good-bye to the bearded man, who was happy enough to leave.

The inside of Louis's trailer was cluttered with newspapers, dirty dishes, and beer cans. He kicked a path to the living area, where a lone recliner sat in front of a television. "Now. What's going on? Why did you come to wake me up?"

"Why did you disappear?" I asked. "You said you were going to be in your tent for the rest of the fair."

"Disappear?" He sat down in his recliner and let out a long sigh. "I just said good-bye to you a few hours ago."

"It's been two days."

He stared at me. "Two days?" He ran a hand over the stubble on his chin and grunted, then looked at his hand as if it had answers. "Impossible."

I shook my head. "No. I came back yesterday to show you to my sister, Kelly. But there was this woman there instead. Genevieve. And she—"

"Genevieve!" Louis surged to his feet. Well, tried to surge. It took three attempts, but he got there at last.

"You know her?" I asked.

"Of course I know her. I trained her, didn't I? I told you to watch out for her!" He pounded his fist against the wall, and the sound boomed through the trailer. "I haven't seen her for eight years. She ran off, and she's been making a mess of things ever since. I'd finally tracked her here . . ." He trailed off, eyes darting around the room.

"She stole my sister's memories of me," I said when Louis didn't speak. "She's forgotten who I am, and she thinks this jerk at school is her boyfriend."

"Genevieve?" Louis asked, not paying attention. He was moving piles of newspaper around, looking underneath them.

"Kelly. My sister."

He nodded, now having moved on to clothes and more cans and frozen dinners. At last he cried out, then emerged with an empty glass bottle. "I was right!"

The bottle didn't seem particularly noteworthy. Just glass. He might want to think about recycling or putting a few fireflies in it, but that's all it was useful for at this point. "Right about what?" I asked.

Louis held the bottle out to me. "Genevieve put me to sleep with this."

"With a bottle?"

"With a memory inside it. Bottled sleep, I'd guess." He sniffed the rim a few times, then licked the edge. "Maybe with a twist of amnesia. Curses!"

"Bottled sleep?"

Louis waved his hand at me in dismissal. "She's mixing

memories. Tweaking them. That's probably how she got your sister to think someone else was her boyfriend. I need to stop her."

"There's a huge line outside her trailer. She set it up in place of your tent."

Louis's jaw dropped. "She—she—she must have come here. Stolen my memories and forced this dose of sleep on me." He hurried to his bedroom. "She must be stopped!" He came out, the robe replaced by pants and an unbuttoned collared shirt. "Help me with my shoes, boy. We'll teach that thief a thing or two." He grabbed his hat from a peg on the wall, and as he took it down, a different bottle fell out of it. Louis caught it and stared at it, his eyes growing wide and the determined look draining from his face.

At first glance, the bottle seemed to be filled with a pale green glow. As soon as Louis touched it, that same color washed over his face, like a mist that was shrouding his eyes. I blinked, and it was gone. Had I imagined it?

Louis gasped and clutched at his left arm. "Oh no." He slumped to the floor in a heap.

I rushed over to kneel by his side. "Louis?"

His mouth opened and closed silently. He spoke. "Your hand. Quickly, boy." He grimaced in pain.

I reached out my hand and put it in his. "I'm—sorry for this," he said. "There's no time, and no—no other way."

Just as I was going to ask what he was sorry for, it hit me. A tsunami of memories and knowledge. Louis as a young boy apprenticing with an older Memory Thief, because that's what they all called themselves. Years of practice, honing his craft. Wandering across Europe after World War II, learning more from other Thieves. Some time with Genevieve. It wasn't every memory Louis had—but it was everything he knew about what he did. How he did it.

My brain couldn't take it all in. I tried to take my hand away, but Louis clutched harder, and the flood of memories increased, coming too fast now for me to catch them all. Flashes of long nights full of study, hours after hours of practice, teachers striking my—his—hands with rulers, a large man beating me—him—when I didn't do it all right. The memory of struggling and wishing it would all end and not knowing if I'd ever be good enough. Pure knowledge, pumped straight into my brain.

My head felt like it was going to explode. Pressure increased behind my eyes, and my vision started to go black. I couldn't breathe. Couldn't think. It was a chore just to remember my name, let alone where I was or what I'd been doing.

I passed out.

When I woke up, I was gasping on the floor, my body drenched in sweat. Above me, three flies buzzed around in random directions, always circling, never landing. In the distance, I could hear the roar of a crowd cheering at one of the events.

After a few minutes, when I could think of anything else, I sat up and looked at Louis.

Sightless eyes stared up at the trailer ceiling. His body was unnaturally still, though his hand still clutched mine in a grip that hadn't loosened. I reached over to pry him off me. "Come on," I said. "Get—"

His skin was already cold to the touch. Stiff. Waxen. I flinched back in surprise and disgust.

Louis was dead.

CHAPTER

7

FILING CABINETS

I ran to get help. I wasn't a doctor, and just because I couldn't find a pulse didn't mean Louis was really gone.

That's how I ended up stuck sitting in the trailer park for two more hours. I was there when the EMTs rushed in, all hurry and panic, and I was there when they walked out, the panic gone. Dead people didn't need panic.

I was there when the policeman came. Police didn't normally control heart attack scenes, but since it happened at the fair, he wanted to check and make sure everything was on the up-and-up.

He had a lot of questions.

What was my relation to Louis? Why was I there to begin with? How did the heart attack start? I tried to answer all of them without lying, but it wasn't easy. For one thing, I doubted he would believe me: I was there because a woman had stolen my twin's memories, and I wanted to get them back? Please. For another, my brain was still frazzled from Louis transferring all those memories to me. I had a hard time thinking straight about anything, let alone which details were okay to share with the policeman and which weren't. It wasn't my fault Louis died, right?

Right.

He was old. It could have happened for any reason. If it was anyone's fault, it was Genevieve's for showing up and messing around with everything. There was that green light right before he'd gasped in pain. Had that been my imagination?

The cop was asking me for the third time where Louis had come from when Louis himself appeared in midair, standing behind the policeman.

I screamed in surprise.

The officer frowned. "What was that for?"

I blinked, ignoring the policeman for the moment. It was Louis, all right. Not glowing in a ghostly manner. Just standing there with his pants pulled too high, still in dire need of some suspenders, and his plaid golf cap jammed on his head. He was staring at the cop and scratching his elbow absent-mindedly.

His death must have upset me even more than I'd thought. How disturbed did a guy have to be to start seeing things?

"Kid?" the cop asked. "You on something?"

I blinked, then did my best to ignore the floating old man. "Oh," I said. "Sorry. I just—"

"You know what?" Louis asked me. "I don't think this gentleman took a shower this morning."

I ignored him, convinced I had gone insane and was hearing and seeing things. "I'm still just upset about him dying," I told the policeman.

"I'm not joking," Louis said. "Look at that patch of hair. I don't think he even combed that."

"I'm sorry, son." The policeman hitched his pants up. He had quite the belly, and there was a spot on his head where his hair had clumped together. "It can be upsetting, I know. Now, what were you saying about where you live?"

I cleared my throat. Lying was one thing. Lying while I was going crazy was even more complicated.

"You're not making me up," Louis said. "I'm not a ghost. And the least that officer could have done would have been to get a comb wet and run it through there a time or two, you know?"

"Will you be quiet?" I snapped.

The policeman frowned. "Excuse me?"

I flushed. "Not you. I—that is—"

"Now you've done it," Louis said. "We're going to have to fix this the hard way."

Stupid ghost.

"I told you," Louis said. "I'm not a ghost. I'm the remnant of my memories. A construct I built in your mind as I was dying. I'll fade in about fifteen minutes, and then you'll be on your own. If I'd known ahead of time I was going to kick the bucket so fast, maybe I could have given you a few days with me." He shrugged. "Water, bridge. There's no way you could have taken ninety-two years of memories at once without going insane. This way, I can give you a fifteen-minute head start, and it won't overwhelm you. Sort of like how going from a hundred miles per hour to stopped is bad if you do it all at once, but just fine if you take it slow. If you listen to me, we'll soon fix this policeman."

"What?" I asked.

The cop was thoroughly confused now. That made two of us.

"I gave you the ability to steal memories," Louis said. "And I'll tell you how to do it."

"—kidding, kid," the policeman was saying. "I think maybe you're in shock."

"How do I do that?" I asked Louis, wishing any of this made sense.

The cop answered first. "You don't go into shock by choice, it's when—"

"Ignore him," Louis said. "We'll take his memories of this encounter in just a second. We can't take many—you have to be careful with memories—but a few small ones won't hurt. First you have to enter his mind."

The policeman was still going, his hands on his waist.

"How?" I asked Louis, not caring where the question fell in the conversation with the policeman. I might have been going insane, but on the off chance that I wasn't, it wouldn't hurt to go along with it. Because being able to take memories on my own . . . I'd be able to solve a lot of problems without needing anyone else's help.

"It happens through eye contact," Louis explained. "All you have to do is catch the gaze of whoever you want to steal from. You know how in stories there are people who can hypnotize you? Just stare in your eyes and *poof*! They're in a trance? That's what Memory Thieves can do."

"—comes a time in everyone's life when they face death head on," the policeman was saying. "And yes, it can be upsetting, but if you can look death straight in the eye—"

Louis continued. "Once you have them in that trance, you dive into their brain. And not really metaphorically, either.

You end up in the middle of a gigantic library. The older the person, the bigger the library, each one with its own style. Memories can be arranged any way you want them. By subject. By date. By place. When you remember where you were on a certain date, you don't have to think about what you were doing that time first. No—your brain goes to the date in question and brings back everything it has for that day. And when you need to know what you learned about algebra last week, you don't have to remember everything about the classroom where you learned it."

"It's like the best Internet search engine ever," I said.

The cop paused, confused. "I don't know if I'd call death a search engine. But . . . I guess that's one way of looking at it."

Louis waved at the man in dismissal. "Enough of this. Look him in the eye and concentrate. Think about having him fall under your trance. The rest will happen automatically."

I stared the policeman in the eye and concentrated.

"Kid?" he said.

I didn't say anything.

"You okay, kid?"

Kept concentrating.

"Are you trying to give me the evil eye?"

He blinked, and I got an intense rushing sensation, as if

I was shrinking and flying forward at the same time, diving into the man's eye and through it into his brain. Everything around me whirled in color and light, and then I was standing in a large room filled with filing cabinets. A lonesome television sat in a corner. Cheap fluorescent lights flickered above me. Louis stood next to me, his face washed out in the bad lighting.

He looked around and sniffed. "The man takes his job too seriously."

Finally, I could listen to Louis without having to have the policeman interrupt. "Where did he go?" I asked.

"You're in his mind. You can read his life. Everything he's ever said, done, thought. Anything."

"What's my body doing?"

"Your body follows through on some reflex actions. It breathes for you. Smiles if you're happy. Grimaces if you're in pain. That sort of thing. But time slows down for Memory Thieves. Ten minutes in here is about ten seconds out there, so you shouldn't generally snoop around in memories when other people are watching. It makes them suspicious. Anyway. All you have to do now is find the memories you want to steal and grab them, then leave by willing yourself out."

My body seemed just as real as ever. Same sneakers. Same jeans. Same T-shirt. Same jacket. Pinching my arm resulted in the same pain, even.

Strange.

I jumped up and down, just to see if I could. The tiles were hard beneath my feet. It was like I was really there. "And no one can tell I'm in here?" I asked. "This is awesome!"

"You grow accustomed to it," Louis said, shrugging. "But we've got other things to take care of. Things like stopping Genevieve and saving your sister. So how about we get this policeman out of the way?"

"What do I do?"

"Walk over to one of those metal filing cabinets. That'll be where he's got his memories. Focus on the kind of memory you want to find, then open the cabinet. Everything you need will be in it."

I went up to a cabinet and concentrated on the first thing that came to my mind: books. Pulling the drawer open, I saw file after file of every book this guy had ever read, arranged in no particular order. There weren't many of them, and most of them were for kids. *Frog and Toad Are Friends.*

Louis shrugged. "We're not all readers."

I closed the drawer and thought of something else.

"Nope," Louis said. "You have to go to another cabinet. Can't use the same one twice."

"Why?" I asked.

"Because it doesn't work. Why else?"

Fair enough. I went to another and focused on fishing,

taking the first thing that popped into my head. It resulted in an entire drawer packed with every fishing-related thing imaginable. Once again, all stuffed in there with no thought for order. There were fishing movies, fishing stories, fishing trips, types of fish, fishing techniques, people he'd fished with. I closed that drawer and focused on fishing trips on Wilson Lake.

When I opened the next drawer, things were more orderly, just as I had expected.

Louis smiled. "You've got a knack for this. That's excellent. The trick with being an ace Memory Thief is to be able to search for very specific things. You could grab all these files and take them out with you, but do you really want all those memories running around in your head?"

"Would that be bad?" I asked.

"Depends."

"On what?"

"On how much you like fishing, I suppose. And your mind's also not up to the task of holding too many memories at once. It might crack under the strain. With practice, you can take on many more. But having just started, you'll want to find your limits first."

"And you're really dead?" I asked.

He sighed. "Unfortunately. Stay focused, though. Let's take his memories of you and then be out of here."

I closed the drawer and went to a different area. This time, I focused on me at the fair today. Just me—exactly how I was looking now. I held my breath and opened the drawer.

It contained a single file folder, with a few sheets of paper inside it.

I examined them. There were notes on what I'd told him so far, including some alarming red circles drawn around the more blatant lies. He hadn't been believing my story, and the longer I'd been talking to him, the more suspicious he'd become.

Life would be much easier for everyone involved if he just forgot I'd ever been at the fair.

I took the entire folder with me, scrunched my eyes closed, and focused on leaving. Once again, there was a rushing sensation, as if I were hurtling backward. And then it stopped, and I opened my eyes.

Louis had disappeared, but the policeman was staring at me. He seemed confused. He blinked a few times and looked around. We were standing across from Louis's trailer, and the ambulance was a pair of taillights in the distance.

"You," the policeman said, staring at me. "You see anything, kid?"

I shook my head and shrugged.

He grunted. "Well, go on. Get out of here. This ain't no place for children."

He walked off, and just like that, I was free. No more questions. Curiously, the memories I'd taken from the policeman were now in my head. I could remember meeting myself. Talking to myself. That was a strange experience—seeing how someone else saw me and what observations they had about me, almost like watching myself on video. Was I really that short?

"Yes," Louis said, popping back into view. "And don't worry about those memories. They're small enough that your mind will absorb them in a minute or two."

"Can't I just . . . destroy it? Rip it up?"

Louis shook his head. "Impossible. It wouldn't work if you tried. The paper won't tear. Memories can't be destroyed, just forgotten, and that usually takes time. But we've got to go over showing memories to other people. Take the officer's hand and focus on drawing him in through that connection. Think of it like . . . sucking his soul into you, just less wicked."

Take his hand? It would probably make sense after I'd done it, just like with jumping into his mind. I hurried back up to the cop and cleared my throat, holding out my hand in an offer to shake. Did I look as awkward as I felt? The cop turned around, gave me a funny stare, but completed the handshake. As soon as our skin touched, I focused on drawing him in. Soul sucking.

But all that was happening was an extended, awkward handshake.

"Come on, kid," Louis said. "Really mean it."

The cop started to pull away, but I gripped harder and focused, and then it worked. Going into someone else's mind had felt like jumping out of my own, but this—drawing someone into my memories—had a feeling more like I was collapsing, as if I were a balloon that was losing all its air.

There was the same whirl of color, and I was in a new library. My bedroom, actually. It had a video game system in a corner, and the walls were lined with free-floating bookshelves attached directly to the walls. It looked like my book collection at home, only much larger. Big books, thin books, fat books, pamphlets—all of them jammed together with no real sense of order or design.

Louis stood in the middle of the room, looking around. "You could really use a good spring cleaning, you know that, kid?"

I shrugged. "It feels pretty cozy to me. Natural."

"Of course it does. It's your mind." Louis jerked his head over at the bed. "And look who you brought with you."

The police officer was lying on the bed, staring at the television. I jumped a little when I saw him. It was the first time I'd seen someone else in one of these places. But he wasn't moving. Wasn't blinking. Wasn't even breathing.

I walked over and waved my hand in front of his face. No response. "What happened to him?"

"That's what people look like when you bring them into your mind. They don't appear when you go into their minds—just when you bring them into yours. Don't worry about him. He's not a Memory Thief. He can't do anything here. But you can. Go over to your shelves and grab a memory that doesn't mean much. Say . . . what you ate for dinner yesterday."

"Same process?" I asked.

"Is the Pope Catholic?"

I sighed, then went over to the shelves and focused on that meat loaf. Taking a thin book down from one shelf at random, I opened it to see a short description of the food. *Kind of dry meat loaf. Needs ketchup.*

"Good," Louis said. "A Memory Thief can't visit his own mind library alone. You need to touch someone else to access it. Now, pay attention. I'm just giving you an overview. What you do with it and why is up to you. There are four parts to Memory Thieving. Copying and stealing—that happens when you go to someone else's mind. Showing and giving— that happens when you bring them to your own place. If you wanted the cop to think he'd eaten that for dinner last night, you could just leave that piece of paper in his hand before you kick him out. Not that I'd recommend it. It would only confuse him. But I want you to get some more practice in before I run out of time. Come on."

Louis blinked out of my memory library, and I followed suit.

The cop finished giving me his strange look, and I let go of his hand. "Thanks for being great," I told him, feeling like I really ought to say something. "And try reading some more."

Without waiting for a response, I turned and left.

Louis was already on the move. Have you ever tried to follow a figment of your imagination? He didn't make it easy on me. He made a beeline for the busiest part of the fair: the midway. It's where all the rides and games were, and while some of us had to actually walk around things to get there, Louis just walked straight through anything in his way. I had to hurry to keep up, and even then, he was scowling at me by the time I made it.

"Pick a person," he said, gesturing to a line of kids waiting outside the Gravitron. "But make it snappy."

I scanned over the line. Erin Worthen was about a third of the way in. I'd known her since forever, and she had nice blonde hair and freckles. My mouth felt cottony, but I walked over to her before I could take too long to think about it.

"Erin," I said. She looked over at me, and with another whirl of color and light, I was in.

The cop's mind had been something straight from a television show. Erin's was a music store complete with instruments. It made sense, in a way. She took private lessons on the French horn. The floor was cherry and the walls were covered with cabinets in the same color. The room was well lit and clean. Instead of the old, dusty television that had been in the policeman's library, this room had a sleek flatscreen on one wall.

Louis was already there, of course. "We've gone over giving memories and stealing memories, but we have to do showing and copying."

"What's the difference?"

Louis groaned and looked at his watch. "We're almost out of time, kid! Think! You know this stuff already. Making a copy of a memory is like recording something in person, just better. But nobody who watches a recording of a birthday party would ever have the whole memory of really being there. The World War II scene I showed to you? Think of the difference between that and the policeman's memory you just erased. With the first one, you watched it, but you still knew you were you. With the second, you couldn't tell the difference between that memory and your own once you'd had it. Right?"

I wanted to stop him. Make him slow down, at least. But his body was beginning to turn transparent. I could watch him vanishing, and the sight left me speechless.

He saw it, too, glancing down and shouting in alarm. "What else? What else? Think, Louis." He snapped his fingers. "The Whispers. Don't forget about the Whispers, and stay well away from them. If you hear them coming, leave at once. But you'd do that anyway, right? Because if they catch you, they'll—"

He disappeared in mid-sentence. One moment he was there, the next I was alone in Erin's mind.

"Louis?" I asked.

No response. I thought he'd said we had fifteen minutes. There was no way that could have been done already. "Louis?" But it was only me in that room.

Whispers? That didn't ring any bells, though it didn't sound like anything I'd want to experience. They'll . . . what? Not make me happy, was my guess. You weren't warned to run and hide from things that made you laugh.

I stayed there for a moment, thinking. If Louis wasn't around to tell me how to do things, then I'd have to figure it out on my own. He'd said I could copy memories. How? I looked around the room for a copy machine or a camera. Nothing. But my gut told me to check out the television, so I strode over to it and turned it on.

A blue screen came up, blank except for *Please Insert Memory* flashing over and over. The words triggered something in my mind. One minute I didn't know what to do, and then I was walking to a cabinet and pulling out the first file that came to mind: vacations.

I scanned over the results. Erin's family had been quite a few places. Yellowstone, Puerto Rico, New York City. It was an impressive list, but "Paris" stood out to me most. I flipped through the pages until I got to the Paris spot and skimmed over them. The Eiffel Tower. That would be a cool memory. Holding onto that piece of paper, I put the others back and went to the television.

When I was a few feet away, the paper began to shine brightly, then leaped out of my hand and onto the screen in front of me. And then I wasn't in Erin's mind anymore. Just like when Louis had shown me the memory of World War II, I was whisked away, first-person-shooter style, into a whole new environment.

It was sunny and hot. Too hot. I was much shorter, with long blonde hair, though I still felt like me. My parents (no, Erin's parents—I recognized them from meetings at school) towered above me, smiling down at me as we came out of a stairwell to a broad square lined with trees. On one side of it, a steady stream of cars zoomed by, filling the air with honks and the constant roar of engines. The opposite side of the square was bordered by a sharp drop-off, lined with a stone wall. We were walking over to it.

When we got closer, I could see over: a broad river, fifty feet wide at least, filled with squat cruise boats lined with people pointing behind me. I turned to see what they were looking at, and there it was: the Eiffel Tower. It was much taller than anything we had in Livingston, Maine. Iron beams crisscrossing like a Lego set on steroids. An elevator was making its way to the top. Tiny dots of people in colorful summer clothes stood on three different levels of the tower.

This wasn't a memory. This wasn't watching something happen. This was living it. I could see the pigeons, smell the trash can off to my right. I could feel the breeze in my hair. As before, I couldn't actually do anything. I couldn't say what I wanted to or go where I wanted to. But short of that, it was just as authentic as seeing the fair had been only moments ago.

I concentrated, flexing an invisible muscle I hadn't known I had, and I was out of the memory again, the piece of paper back in my hand.

A smile broke across my face. Copying memories. Piece of cake. Showing memories had to be similar. Bring someone into my personal memory library and put my own memory up on the screen there. They'd experience it at the same time I did. All of this was making sense. Mostly.

The day had started off about as bad as I could imagine. Kelly's memories were messed up, Genevieve was wreaking havoc on my town, and I'd been as helpless as could be.

Now?

It was like I'd been staring at an impossible problem for hours, and then someone waltzed in and handed me the answer key. I could take memories. See memories. Use memories. I felt the knowledge there in my mind, waiting for me to explore it, and the confusion and fear I'd felt this morning was replaced by an overwhelming feeling of confidence and excitement.

I was going to find Kelly and fix her, and then?

Genevieve was going to pay.

CHAPTER

8

SCUBA DIVING

When you've just been given the keys to a brand-new car, you don't stick that car in a garage and ignore it. (At least, that's what it seemed like from TV.) You drive it around.

I debated hanging around Erin's for a bit longer to . . . snoop, but it felt wrong. Rude. So I jumped out of her and decided to stick with strangers instead.

When I was out of Erin's head, I was back outside the Gravitron, gawking at her. "What?" she asked.

I blinked, my mind racing to come up with something to say. "Have you seen Sam anywhere?"

She frowned. "Sam? No."

"Okay, thanks." I turned and hurried off, feeling sheepish. Still, I could go back and swipe that memory from her if I wanted to, and that thought helped brighten me up. I never had to be embarrassed again.

I searched for another person. Not a girl this time. That had been strange. I wanted someone with lots of memories. Something exciting and different, that I'd never seen before. Most of the people there were young, but there was an older gentleman sitting in a wheelchair by one of the french fry houses, waiting for someone. He was perfect. He must have lived through all sorts of things. The Great Depression, maybe, or he might have been a spy during the Cold War, or something even better. I cleared my throat, and he glanced up at me. I just needed a second of eye contact to—

His mind library was something you'd find in a five-million-dollar mansion. Not cavernous, though. Compact and luxurious. All leather-bound books and polished mahogany bookshelves. A fireplace crackled to one side, with an easy chair positioned right by it, perfect for a nice evening of reading. On the opposite wall, an old-fashioned projector was pointed at a blank screen.

Time to get cracking.

I walked over to a shelf and ran my fingers across the books. The leather was cool to the touch. What did I want to see? Hard to tell without knowing him. I'd let him decide instead. Focusing on "Most Exciting Experience," I pulled out a book at random, wondering what I'd find. A trip through the Himalayas? Another war scene?

I didn't want to know ahead of time. Let it be a surprise. I took the book over to the projector, which whirred to life as I approached, the gears moving and the light turning on to cast a stark beam on the screen in front of it. The book flashed in my hands, heating my fingers for a moment and then . . .

Underwater. I glanced above me, my vision obscured by goggles, but the surface could still be seen, shimmering somewhere in the distance. My focus turned back on my surroundings. I was in a cage in the middle of endless blue.

"We're tossing in the chum bucket now," a voice said to me through an ear piece. "Get ready for some action."

My breath increased, adrenaline flowing through my body. What was a chum bucket, and why did that make me—

A large bucket plunged down from above, streaking through the water, trailing a jet of white bubbles and red coloring. Was that blood? A large something flashed by me in the corner of my eye. My body turned to catch a glimpse of it, but there was no need to catch anything.

Sharks.

Everywhere I looked. Huge, massive, powerful bodies darting in and out of view. I turned my head just in time to see an enormous mouth full of razor-sharp teeth slash at the bars of my cage. Thank goodness I was protected, but why in the world was I down there with all these sharks to begin with?

Another shark struck the cage, though I could only hear a faint clanging sound through the water. For as violent as things were getting out there, it was surprisingly quiet. The bars shook again. Maybe the sharks were wishing they had something a little more meaty.

"You getting this?" the voice asked.

My hands fumbled at my chest, bringing a camera in front of me. So that's what I was up to. I was a photographer. Long ago, judging by how much younger this body was compared to the old man whose memory I was experiencing. I took some time to enjoy the moment: the cool pressure of the water around me, the sights of the shark feeding frenzy, the noise of my breath coming in slow parcels, in and out.

Another shark hit the cage, its teeth chomping at the bars only a foot from my face. Come to think of it, the bars didn't seem nearly as strong as they ought to be. This was decades ago. Were shark cages as safe back then?

Just as I thought the question, an enormous monster of a

shark rushed straight at the cage, mouth wide and with all the speed it could muster. It hit with a shuddering blow, and the bars bent. Bent! The beast worked its way at the bars, struggling to get closer to me.

My breath was coming in gasps now. I pressed up against the back of the cage, only to have a different shark attack me from there.

A shadow passed above me, and I looked up to find yet another shark chewing at the cable that attached the cage to the boat. Nothing could bite through that, though. Right? I had to be—

The cable snapped.

The cage did what any giant piece of metal would do in the ocean. It sank. Deeper and deeper. I was going to die. My mind was a panicked mess. I wasn't prepared for this. What were you supposed to do? If I went out there, the sharks would devour me, but if I stayed, who knew how far down I'd go? Wouldn't the pressure squash me flat?

But while I might have been panicking, the man whose memory this was had stayed relatively calm. He looked up, then down, then up again, and then without another moment of hesitation, he opened the top of the cage and dove through, letting it continue on its way to the watery depths below. The man—I—used strong strokes of my arms and stronger lunges from my flippered feet to hurry to the surface as fast as I could.

Sharks were everywhere. I ignored them, even as I recognized that any moment one might come at me. Still, my breaths rang out individually in my ears. In and out. In and out. The surface was closer. Twenty feet? A shark lunged at me, and I paused long enough to punch it in the nose as hard as I could. It veered off.

I kept swimming,

And then I'd broken the surface.

Hands reached out for me while others punched out at any shark that came close. I'd been weightless and free under the water, but now that I was out, I was all flippers and oxygen tanks. I felt about a thousand pounds too heavy. The boat seemed impossible to get into, and I kept waiting for my arm to disappear, replaced by a bloody stump.

But somehow, I made it in.

I ripped off my mask and scuba gear and lay there, gasping, watching the faces of the stunned men around me while in the background the noise of the feeding frenzy continued.

And then I began to laugh. It was a man's laugh, low and loud and happy as any I'd ever heard. With that sound, the rest of the crew joined in, almost like a spell had been broken. The danger was gone, and I was still alive. I'd never felt that aware of myself before.

With a blink, I was back in the man's mind library, staring down in wonder at the leather book in my hands again. That had been incredible.

I wasn't going to stop there, of course. I wanted more. More experiences. More adventures. Why not take a moment to get really familiar with how it all worked? Besides, the old man I was visiting had more than enough memories to go around.

"Benjamin," whispered a soft voice, so quiet I almost missed it.

I turned, looking for where the sound had come from. The room was empty. Had I imagined it? Probably. Louis had warned me to watch for Whispers, and so I was inventing some right on cue. Shaking my head, I turned back to focus on the next memory I wanted to experience. Another boat voyage? More diving? Maybe something from earlier in his childhood.

"Benjamin."

The whisper had been louder now. I was sure of it. I turned again and studied the far wall. Was it just me, or had the room . . . tilted a little? Just for a moment.

"Come here," the whisper said. "Here to the corner."

Most people, when they heard a mysterious voice whisper to them in an empty room, would do the sensible thing and get out of that room. That's what my mind was telling me—screaming at me—right then. Jump out of there and go somewhere else.

But most people hadn't heard that voice. Heard those whispers.

It said to come to the corner, and all I wanted to do was obey. Go to the corner and see what it wanted show me. Why *shouldn't* I go to the corner? There was nothing there to harm me. Nothing to be worried about. It was just an empty corner.

Better to not think about it at all. Just do what the voice told me.

I went over to the corner. The light didn't quite reach over here. It was darker. Shadowed.

"Put your face up to the bookshelf," the whisper said.

Again, sort of a strange request, but why not give it a shot? That voice made sense. It was only reasonable. The bookshelf was made out of wood. Inanimate. It wasn't going to hurt me. And even though my common sense was hollering and waving its arms at me, it was too easy to just do what the whisper had asked me to.

I put my face up against the bookshelf.

"Good," it said. "Now. Listen."

I stayed there for several heartbeats, my face flush with one of the shelves, the wood's grain smooth on my cheek. What was I listening for? Would it be a surprise? Maybe Louis had never actually seen who Whispered. He was old. Old people were scared. There couldn't be—

Arms of shadow thrust out of the bookshelf, clamping down on either side of my head. They might have looked as insubstantial as smoke, but there was power in them. They gripped my head and shoved it back, then brought it smashing into the shelf, right on the bridge of my nose.

My vision went white. The pain was unbearable. I lunged back, trying to escape, but the grip was too strong. One hand clutched at my hair while the other let go to rain blows on my face, my ears, my shoulders. Each one with the force of a heavyweight.

I screamed and clawed at the arm, but I might as well have tried to escape from a hunk of granite.

"You don't belong here!" the Whisper cried out. "Unnatural. Evil. Wicked! You're a failure. Pitiful. Betrayer. Pretender!"

Each word cut me deeper than the blows. They were true, every one. My twin was in trouble, and here I was, playing with shark memories. I should just submit to the blows. Give in. Give up.

In front of me, a face appeared, dark and shadowy, with only two pinpricks of red embers of light for eyes. It opened its mouth far wider than any natural thing could have, revealing row upon row of razor-sharp teeth, inches from my eyes.

Its breath smelled of rotting flesh and the inside of abandoned tombs. Decay and ruin and despair. Of long lonely nights that waited for everyone. Because sooner or later, we were all left alone. Our friends and family would die, and there would be no one else who cared for us. Who could comfort us. And wasn't I better giving up now rather than struggling for no good reason?

And I was almost convinced. I was inches away from stopping my struggles and giving in, but right before I did, something inside me snapped, and I realized I could leave this man's memory library behind. And as soon as I thought of it, I leaped clear and was back in my own body, screaming and blinking and gasping in the afternoon air.

The old man stared at me in confusion. It wasn't every day someone glanced at you and then cried out in terror the next moment. I looked around me. The crowd had all frozen, gawking at me. Now that I was back at the fair, my mind returned enough to realize I should hurry off somewhere private. Blushing as red as could be, I tucked my head down and scampered away, leaving the crowd behind and heading to the back side of a doughnut cart a safe distance from where I'd just made a scene.

When I got there and no one was looking, I collapsed to the grass and stayed there, staring at nothing and feeling my face for any damage *whatever it was* might have left behind.

But there was nothing there. Nothing but the memory of how close I came to giving up, and how powerless I'd been to stop that thing. The Whispers. So that's what they were. It had seemed like the longer I'd stayed in that mind, the stronger they'd gotten. And once I'd started paying attention to them, it had gotten harder and harder to stop.

It had been a close call, but now that I knew what to expect, I'd do better at resisting them.

At the same time, I was shaken. The thought of going back into someone's mind and coming face-to-face with one of those things was more than enough to make me want to just take a long walk and cool down instead.

What if they were waiting for me next time? What if once you'd started listening to the Whispers, it became that much easier for them to get you to listen to them again? And the more you hopped in and out of memory libraries in a short period of time, the worse they got?

All things considered, it would be better for me to take some time to adapt to this new ability. Maybe make a rule for myself: no jumping into more than four or five memory libraries a day.

That sounded about right.

Safer, at least. And right now, safer felt really good.

CHAPTER

9

THE COMPUTER TERMINAL

After cowering behind the doughnut cart for ten minutes or so, I stood, brushed myself off, and went to find a phone. I needed to get home so I could fix Kelly, or at least try to.

However, I hadn't gone more than fifty feet before I stopped dead in my tracks. You'd think after all the surprises today had thrown at me, I'd be through with them. That there couldn't be any way for yet another new thing to assault me.

You'd think wrong.

I was staring at a man in front of me. There was nothing noteworthy about him: tall, brown hair, dressed in jeans and a T-shirt. I mean, he had a slightly confused look on his face, as if he'd forgotten his car keys and wasn't quite sure where to begin to find them. If that was all, he wouldn't have stood out from the crowd.

But it wasn't.

He was normal, with one exception: his eyes were completely black. I don't mean his pupils were dilated, or he was drugged, I mean every bit of his eye—anything that got covered up when he blinked—was black as sin.

What was it? I thought at first it was some strange contact lenses he was wearing. Something covering his eyes. But as I kept walking, I saw a second. Then a third. I counted thirty-five people whose eyes were completely black, and then I gave up. They weren't blind: they could still see. This was something only someone like me could detect. But they'd had core memories ripped away from them, and they would never be able to recover on their own. Beyond the ones with eyes completely dark were countless others who had black splotches peppered across their eyes like someone who'd taken a Dalmatian theme too literally.

No one else was staring at them strangely. No one but me noticed, though all the people with black eyes looked more confused than normal. Lost somehow, and I could guess why.

Genevieve.

She'd been stealing memories from these people. It was

the only thing that made sense, and my instincts said my guess was right. All those memories from Louis were kicking around my head, seeping over into my memory. From what I could piece together from them, a mind was like a river running through a valley. It had its way of doing things and was used to the routine. Remove a key bend in the riverbank, and who knew which direction the river might end up going. That's why you only took memories when people offered them to you. A person's mind could prepare itself for the loss of a memory. Do some major construction on the riverbanks ahead of time, if that made sense.

Take too much, and the personality didn't just change, it crumbled. And when that happened, their eyes began to go black. Not all at once, and not uniformly. Imagine your pupils were an inkwell, and someone sloshed that ink around. Black lines and splotches would extend from the pupils, making a person's eyes look like they had been painted black by a three-year-old. The more a person was affected, the more black lines appeared.

This problem wasn't just about Kelly, it was about the whole town, and I was the only one who could do anything about it.

I tried to jump into the minds of one of these people, picking a middle-aged man in a Red Sox cap and polo shirt. His eyes were totally black, like someone had dipped each eyeball in paint. You couldn't help but squirm when you looked at him. So much of a person rests in their eyes: their emotions, their thoughts. Talk to someone in sunglasses, and you understand that. It's hard to tell what they really mean. See what they're thinking. This was a whole lot worse.

Could I fix him? Help him some way? I wanted to give it a try, but as soon as I went to dive into his mind, it was like I'd hit a brick wall, literally. My head erupted in pain, and I stumbled back and fell to the ground, attracting quite a few stares in the process.

I shook my head and waved off the couple of people who'd come to see what the problem was. The man in the Red Sox cap had put a hand to his head and frowned, as if he'd experienced some pain, too.

So apparently jumping in wasn't an option. It would have been helpful to know that *before* I dove into a solid wall, of course.

What if I couldn't get into Kelly's mind to fix her? A pit formed in my stomach. If I had this ability given to me, and I still couldn't solve things, then I was really hopeless. It's not like I could expect any more help than this. I'd been lucky as it was.

I had to get home. Had to see Kelly and try this out. If it didn't work, then I'd go to Genevieve. Confront her. Make her fix it.

Somehow.

I called my dad from a pay phone, and after he got through yelling at me for being at the fair again, he told me he was on his way to pick me up. I waited outside the fairgrounds, safely away from Genevieve. I didn't want her knowing what had happened to me.

At the same time, I was also trying to work through a problem in my head—the problem that had started this whole mess.

My parents.

Even if I got Kelly back to normal, would it matter if my parents really decided to divorce? What if they split us up? When I'd first heard them talk about it, I couldn't think of a thing I could do to stop it.

Now I had this new ability. Didn't it make sense to put it to use?

But then I remembered those people with their eyes all darkened and the confused looks on their faces. What if my parents ended up like that? And even if I didn't go that far, stealing memories could have consequences you couldn't foresee.

That thought held me up for a while. But then it occurred to me. What if I just . . . *borrowed* the memories? Took them out for a while, just to see what kind of an effect it had on my parents. That couldn't hurt, could it? Louis's memories seemed to tell me it was more complicated than that, but he was old. Old people were always so hesitant. So afraid.

And he hadn't had to deal with his parents hating each other.

At last, Dad's red Subaru pulled up to the curb.

My father yelled at me right away, his voice booming in the small car. He was in fine form, talking about a lack of responsibility and a need to grow up. It was enough to give a kid ideas. I wouldn't take all his memories of his arguments with Mom (probably), but I could at least go in and rip up the ones he had that were making him so angry at me, couldn't I?

He took a deep breath and started a new line of attack. "I know we let you get away with—"

"Dad," I said, making up my mind. We were stopped at a red light. Louis was too cautious, and I'd be really careful. Even the memory of the Whispers wasn't enough to stop me. I'd be in and out. Fast.

"What?"

"Look at me."

He took his eyes off the light for a second.

That was all I needed.

With a *whoosh*, I was in his memories. Dad's mind was much different than the other libraries I'd been in so far. Instead of cracked tile and flickering fluorescents, his was a cramped room with a computer and an industrial printer. No paintings or decorations. Just white walls, gray carpet, and strong office lights over a cheap desk and chair.

I paused for a moment, listening. No voices. No Whispers. I had to move quickly, though. Didn't want to chance them showing up again. I walked over and pulled out the chair—a pleather seat on roller wheels—and sat at the desk, doing my best to dismiss my unease. Louis had been old and scared. These were real problems I had, and I could fix them.

Assuming I could figure out how to search Dad's memories. There were no cabinets, but there was a basic search box on the screen and an "Enter" button next to it. Could it be that easy?

I typed *reasons to be mad at Benji Lewis* and today's date, then hit "Return."

The printer whirred to life, shooting out two pages of bullet points ranging from me lying about where I'd been to me having not cleaned my room.

I gripped the sheets firmly in my hand, then concentrated on leaving.

In a blink, I was back in the Subaru. Dad glanced at me. "What was I saying?" he asked.

I knew full well what he'd been saying. I could remember being angry at me. In fact, part of me really *was* angry at me. How could I have lied like that? Didn't I know better? But

I knew those were just my dad's memories kicking around with my own, and I did my best to squelch them.

"You were telling me about your day," I said to Dad.

"I was?"

I nodded. And just like that, he launched into a summary of what he'd been up to. Not a trace of anger toward me. I studied him while he talked. He didn't seem hurt in any way. Definitely happier, no trace of black around the eyeballs. And the memory I'd taken from him wasn't doing anything bad to me. Plus, there hadn't been even a trace of the Whispers. I'd been completely safe.

So why was my heart pounding so hard, and why was I dreading going back in?

"How's Mom?" I asked Dad. Better to know the lay of the land before we got home.

"Fine," he said curtly.

So it was no better. At the next light, I made another quick decision, doing my best not to think about it too much. Sorry, heart rate. This had to be done. "Dad?"

"What?"

"Look at me," I said.

"Again?"

"Just for a sec."

In a blink, I was back at the computer terminal. This time I'd do a more powerful search. *Reasons I'm angry at my wife.*

I had a fair idea what to expect before I ran the search: stuff about Mom not getting a job. Twenty sheets tops. But even spitting out two pages per second, it took a lot of waiting until the printer was done.

Three minutes in, it happened.

A voice, soft and insistent, coming from the far corner of the room. "Come to the corner, Benjamin."

I blinked and shook my head. If I didn't pay any attention, then I wouldn't have anything to worry about. And while there might have been a few more muffled whispers from that corner, I managed to keep things under control.

At the end, I had a stack of papers a foot high. I'd known Mom and Dad didn't get along, but this was crazy. Just looking at random, I saw lists of times Mom had criticized Dad. Times she'd been running too slow. A huge list of times she spent too much money or commented about how little money he made. Times when she'd belittled him or ignored him. I could probably piece together what went wrong in their marriage—how things got to be as bad as they were. But it would take forever, and from the look of things, it was all Mom's fault, and it was much more than money.

How could she have done all this?

Dad would feel better once he wasn't carrying around that baggage. Wouldn't it be better if I just ripped it up right now?

He didn't need all this. It was making him miserable. But the memory of those people with black spots in their eyes stopped me. If I ripped the memories up, I couldn't get them back. I'd just take them for now, and when I knew for sure Dad was okay without them, then I'd rip them up.

But still I hesitated. This was an awful lot of memories for me to be taking on at once. Was I up to it? A big part of me wanted to abandon this, but if I did nothing, my parents' fighting would only get worse, and I was the only person in a position to fix this.

I took the files, closed my eyes, and went back to my body.

There was my dad driving again. "What was it?" he asked.

"Nothing," I said. "I'm beat. Can I rest?"

He let me be, but I wasn't tired. I was overwhelmed. My mother. Zoe. I remembered everything I'd taken with me from my dad's memories. All the slights. And they weren't abstract. They were personal. She'd done them to *me*. Like when she'd made fun of me in the middle of the company party, right in front of my boss. Sure, she'd said she hadn't meant it to come off that way, but that was just a line. She had it in for me. She wanted me to feel like an idiot.

The woman was vindictive as sin, and I'd been stuck with her for over fifteen years.

No—that wasn't right. It wasn't me. I had to keep that in check. But how? I tried telling myself to focus on something else. What I'd had for breakfast that morning. What I'd learned in Social Studies. But my mind kept returning to all the things my wife had done to me. How dismissive she was of me.

My hands balled into fists, and I clenched my jaw. I'd tell her what I thought of her the moment we were home. Let her really have it. And then I'd leave her tonight. Check into a motel and worry about my stuff later. Let the lawyers work through that.

Enough was enough.

A part of me—a quiet part of Louis's experience—told me these weren't my memories. I'd just taken on way too much of one specific emotion, and I didn't have enough experience of my own to counterbalance it. But maybe I could, if I focused hard enough. If I kept reminding myself that these memories weren't mine. They were my father's. Not my thoughts. His thoughts.

Not my thoughts. His thoughts. That was right. It took some focus, but I managed to suppress the anger I felt toward my mom. Most of it, at least. And anyway, I had reasons to be angry with her. The way she bossed me around. Nitpicked my decisions.

But she was my mom, not my wife.

Repressing the memories felt like carrying a big stone. It

took effort, but I could do it. I mentally thanked Louis. That had been a close call. Should I return the memories? I studied Dad's eyes, looking for any traces of spots. How much did a Memory Thief have to do to make those appear? However much it was, I hadn't gotten there, it seemed. Dad's eyes were spot-free.

Still, I knew from Louis's memories that taking too much of a person's memory could warp their personality. A man could go from being an avid fisherman who loved lazy Sunday afternoons to a frenetic businessman who never wasted a moment. Happy people became chronically depressed, funny people became morose. It wasn't always bad (morose people sometimes ended up happy), but you couldn't know what it would do.

I'd hold on to the memories and wait and see.

The rest of the car ride home was silent. Dad let me rest, since he didn't have any reason to yell at me anymore. As far as he was concerned, he'd just come to pick me up from the fair. I had plenty to worry about.

Dad now had no memory of ever being mad at Mom, but she had plenty of memories of being mad at him. If he came home and she launched into her "I'm mad at you" routine, that would ruin everything. I'd started this. Shouldn't I finish it?

But I was already lugging around all of Dad's memories,

and it was almost all I could do to keep them constrained. They pulled at my mind like an angry dog tugging on a leash. As long as I focused, I could keep them in check, but I kept finding myself fuming about something Zoe—no, *Mom*—had done years ago.

Could I really handle Mom's memories, too?

Why had I done this now? Couldn't it have waited until after I'd solved Kelly's problem? I'd been too impulsive. If I gave the memories back to Dad, then . . .

He'd go back to being angry. And Louis's experience chimed in (late as always): taking memories out and switching them around too much was bad for the memories. I'd started this. I ought to finish it.

Dad shouted out as soon as we came in, "Honey! I'm home!"

Cheesy, but way better than the silence and slammed door he often had ready when he got back.

Mom and Kelly were upstairs making dinner, and Mom strode to the top of the stairs to yell at Dad. "Well? What took you so long?"

I glared back and made up my mind. No time to think about if it was the right decision. It was the *only* decision after what I'd done with Dad. With another *whoosh*, I was in her memory library. Mom's was a copy of the local ski lodge. I knew she used to go skiing back when we were younger, but

I had no idea it was still that important to her. The fireplace was crackling in the middle of the room, and the walls were lined with cubbyholes for ski boots and equipment, except these cubbies all had doors instead of being open like in real life.

My stomach felt like it did right before a pop quiz I wasn't prepared for. Could I really go through with this? If I didn't, Mom was going to yell at Dad. She'd ruin everything I'd just done. I had to *fix* this. Besides, most of the problem had to be Mom. I'd tidy up the few complaints she had about Dad, and that would be that.

But even as I thought that, I knew this wouldn't work. Who knew what I'd done to my father already, or what I'd done to myself. Memories were like an ocean, deep and mysterious. Take out some water from one part, and other water rushed in to fill it. Add more water to the ocean, and it swirled in unexpected ways.

On the other hand, I told myself, I'd added years of my dad's memories to my own, and I needed memories to counterbalance them. Stealing Mom's could do the trick. Right?

"Benjamin," a Whisper came. "Listen to me for a moment."

No more thinking. Time for doing.

I opened a cubby door. It was filled with filing boxes, some of them battered and worn out, some of them fresh and new.

So many, and all of them stuffed with memories.

Everything from what Mom ate for dinner five years ago to how her father's breath smelled Christmas morning when she was five. A mind remembers every detail. All of it stored, waiting for retrieval. But we go through our lives focusing only on the important memories. How a person's breath smelled didn't matter—not unless it led to something bigger, like an argument.

I focused on "reasons I'm mad at Benji today" and took out a folder from one of the boxes. It only contained a few pieces of paper. I checked to make sure they were what I was after: *Didn't clean his room* was written on one in my mom's neat handwriting. I flipped to another: *Lied about where he was after school.*

Mom was all about being short, sweet, and to the point. So were her memories.

"There's something over here you should see," the Whispers said.

I needed to hurry. Because part of me wondered what it was they wanted to show me, and that couldn't be a good sign. I took out the papers and put the box back, empty.

Now for the harder part. I went to a new cabinet and focused on "reasons I'm angry with my husband."

When I opened the cubby door, a sea of boxes burst to the floor. In fact, the boxes fell out, and more kept coming, until a quarter of the lodge floor was covered in papers, all with neat dates and statements on them. *Didn't eat the dinner I cooked. Refused to clean the dishes. Walked in muddy boots across my mopped floor.*

But again, the more I looked through the papers, the more I saw things more complicated than dirty dishes. Forgotten birthdays. Disparaging remarks about Grandma. Ignoring Mom at parties. Long nights at work. As I read them, I discovered Dad had been just as much to blame for this mess as Mom. I felt bad that I'd judged her so harshly.

Still, it didn't matter. They'd all be gone for her in a few minutes, and then I'd just repress them on my own. Sure, there were more than I'd planned, but it would work out.

"Listen to me for a moment, Benjamin."

No. Stay focused. Almost done.

I crouched on the floor and gathered the papers into some semblance of order. Free from their boxes, they were a stack at least two feet high.

Once I had something like a neat pile, I steeled myself, and then I was back in my body, looking at my mom. She smiled at us. "Welcome back, you two! I wondered when you would show up."

My dad. No—my conniving, lazy, good-for-nothing husband. No—father. Wasn't he? But all I could remember were the awful times. How he'd questioned my credit card bill last month, despite the fact that he'd bought a new grill just earlier that week. How he would ignore the entire family so he could sit in front of a television and watch the Red Sox. How he made me feel guilty every time he went off to his new job. The man had yelled at me—*yelled* at me—for spending too much on groceries. And not in private, either. In the middle of back-to-school night. I'd been mortified, and that wasn't the least of it. Everything was there. The fights we'd had. The arguments when—I checked myself. Those were Mom's memories, not my own. *Remember that, Benji. Remember.*

Now I was "carrying" the equivalent of two heavy rocks. It took a lot of concentration and focus, but I managed it.

More or less. I was sure I'd get better at it with time and practice.

Some of it was from the fact that the memories generally balanced themselves out. Mom and Dad had different recollections of the same event. It was hard to be as white-hot angry when you had distinct memories of both sides of the argument. Mom hadn't meant to make fun of Dad at that party in front of his boss. I'd—*she'd*—just made a silly attempt at a joke, and it had backfired. And then he'd completely overreacted, just like he always did.

We had an interesting evening. Kelly had apparently gone straight to her room when she came home. She wasn't talking to anyone, but my parents didn't seem to care. They were getting along better than I'd ever remembered. Smiling at each other. Making excuses to touch each other. It was like they were newlyweds, and more than a little disgusting. If Kelly wanted to abandon me to stick with these two, then she deserved whatever rough patch she was going through. Had I been worried about her earlier? Why?

Dad asked Mom how her day was, and they had a normal conversation about work and chores. No veiled insults. No avoiding certain topics. I know that makes it sound like my parents had been fighting constantly for as long as I could remember, and that's not quite what I mean. Life at our house hadn't been one long argument. It had been a series of big arguments, with long cease-fire agreements in between.

This evening was different. It was like when you get used to hearing a certain noise—the hum of your refrigerator, say. And that noise is there all the time, until you get to the point where you no longer even hear it. You could be in a room and think everything's quiet. But when the noise *stops*, you realize how loud it had been all along, and you see what real silence is like.

This was that, but with arguments.

Too bad I couldn't enjoy it.

Dad scraped his teeth on his fork with every bite. He knew that irritated me; I'd told him that for the past eighteen years. And Mom was chewing with her mouth open half the time.

How many times had I told her to stop that? I told myself I was just grumpy because of the memories I'd stolen. But I was repressing those memories like a champ. I was sure of it.

Maybe I was just tired.

The longer the dinner went on, the more I realized something else: Mom and Dad were ignoring Kelly and me. Not completely pretending we didn't exist, but . . . not asking how my day was. Not wondering what was wrong with Kelly. Not checking to see if I was eating enough food, or minding my manners. I didn't expect to be waited on nonstop at dinner, but I also expected to be part of the conversation. And for the love of all that was good in this world, if my dad scraped his fork on his teeth *one more time*, I was going to take that fork and ram it down his throat.

Finally, I excused myself and went to my room, not even waiting for them to give me permission. It didn't matter. They hardly noticed I'd left. I stomped upstairs and hesitated in front of Kelly's door. Should I knock?

Part of me remembered thinking it was important, but the bigger part of me just didn't care. Kelly was a big girl. She got herself into this mess. Let her stew for a while. She deserved it.

I went to my room and lay down, staring at the ceiling. Why was I so angry?

It had to be because I still hadn't fixed things for Kelly.

Though why *I* should be the one who had to fix everything was beyond me. Couldn't the girl do something by herself for once? Whatever. If I could just solve that problem, I'd be able to enjoy happy parents.

Parents who ignored me now that they had each other to focus on.

It didn't matter. Tomorrow, everything would be better.

CHAPTER

10

LIQUID HATE

The next morning, Mom and Dad had disappeared from the house. Dad was usually showering. Mom would be fixing breakfast or getting the house ready for cleaning later in the day. This morning?

Silence.

The Subaru was missing from the driveway. No note to explain where they'd gone. I tried calling them. No answer. I couldn't believe it. The pair of them were every bit as rotten as their memories of each other said they were. If Kelly or I tried a stunt like that, Mom and Dad would be livid. Well, the Mom and Dad of the day before yesterday would have been.

This was from what I'd done. I knew it instinctively. And if taking the memories had done this, couldn't I fix it by putting them back? Of course I could. Memories knew where they belonged. If I brought Mom or Dad into my mind library, I could unload all this garbage and give it back to the people who deserved it.

They just had to show up long enough for me to do that.

I was grumpy when I went in to wake up Kelly. She was lying in the middle of her bed, arms sprawled to the side. I poked her on her shoulder. "Hey," I snapped. "Get up. You're going to be late."

She groggily opened one eye and groaned, then caught sight of me and screamed.

I jumped back a few feet and looked behind me, thinking maybe someone had snuck in. The room was empty.

"You!" Kelly yelled. "Get out! Get out!"

"What?" I asked.

"You're just—just some elaborate prank my parents are playing on me. I came home and they'd photoshopped your picture all over the house. It's not funny!"

Oh. Right. I sighed. "Come on, Kelly. This is ridicu—"

She threw a shoe at my head. That was it. I snapped. "You want to pretend I don't exist? Fine. Whatever. You little snot." I saw her keys to the house on the floor, bent down, and picked them up. "I'm taking these and locking the door on our way out. You want to get back in tonight, you're going to admit I'm your brother."

I stormed out of the room and slammed the door. My twin was an idiot. My parents were morons. The whole world was a waste of my time.

My day didn't get better from there. I wolfed down some cereal and then had to endure a long wait for the bus while Kelly ignored me. She had her arms folded and her eyes were red, still very upset from this "prank" our now nonexistent parents had pulled on her. Not that she didn't deserve whatever mental anguish she was going through. She thought she was Sam Hyde's girlfriend, after all. And she'd made me feel like a loser at school. Sure, I could have tried to sneak into her mind and see if I couldn't fix things or find out what was wrong, but why bother?

She deserved some red eyes.

The bus driver drove way too slowly, lurching up to speed at a snail's pace and then jamming on the brakes at each stop. The other kids on the bus were too loud, yelling at each other about the fair and talking excitedly about Genevieve's booth. One guy in the middle of the bus told everyone else—loudly—that his parents had told him to stay well away from that booth. The rest of them proceeded to make fun of him.

I whirled in my seat and glared behind me at all of them.

"Genevieve is a thief and a liar. Are the rest of you too dense to realize that?"

They all snickered. Somebody hit me in the head with a spitball. I leaped out of my seat and ran to the back of the bus, fists flying. There was a prolonged scuffle, and the next thing I knew, the bus driver was pulling me off George Noel, a thirteen-year-old kid who lived farther down the road.

He had a bloody nose.

He deserved it, I was sure of it. But the bus driver had the nerve to blame me for everything. He made me come sit at the front, and when I told him what I thought of that, he made me go to the principal's office as soon as we got to school.

I'd never been to the principal's. Not once in my life. A row of chairs sat outside his office. Not many. Our school wasn't that big, after all. I was the only kid there, staring at the oak door with "Mr. Waturi" written in block letters next to it.

I wondered why today of all days I had something like this happen to me, but then the principal called me in.

"Benji," he said, his hands folded in his lap as he sat on the edge of his desk. "Having a bad day?"

"No," I answered.

"Care to tell me what happened on the bus?"

"A bunch of idiots were doing what they do best. Being

idiots. So I told them to stop. They didn't like that, so they got what was coming to them."

Mr. Waturi raised his eyebrows, then glanced at a piece of a paper on his desk. "And that meant punching one of them and . . . head-butting another?"

"I should have gotten more of them," I said. "Little weasels."

His mouth dropped open.

"You trying to catch flies, you imbecile?" I said. "You need a lesson, too?"

"Benjamin—" he started.

I didn't let him finish. "Your school sucks, did you know that? Your teachers are half-wits, your students make *Lord of the Flies* look like day camp, and the food tastes like my gym shorts."

I went on from there, which is how I got detention for five days. I stole his memory of giving it to me, naturally. The principal's mind was a duplicate of his office, just with more filing cabinets. The guy was hyper-organized, though. Where the cop's filing cabinets had been crammed and haphazardly thrown together, each drawer I opened of Mr. Waturi's mind was meticulously arranged, with every piece of paper placed just so, and all the folders labeled and easy to read.

Part of me wanted to do something mean while I was in there. Steal a memory he valued. But it would have been too much work. Instead, I focused on "memories from this morning," and ripped up the whole folder without paying attention to what was in it.

Mr. Waturi was looking dazed and befuddled when I left his office, seething. This was all Genevieve's fault. If she hadn't messed around with Kelly, then I wouldn't have gone back to confront her. Louis would still be alive, and I wouldn't have a bunch of my parents' memories zooming around.

Through a great deal of self-restraint, I managed to not make a return visit to the principal's office that day. My main approach was to not open my mouth unless I was asked a direct question, and when that happened, I answered in as few words as possible.

Kelly was still a jerk. Laughing with her new moron friends and pretending I didn't exist.

Good riddance. Who needed a twin anyway? I could get by just fine on my own. My parents were complete failures. I didn't need any family. What I needed was to get back at the world. At anyone who irritated me, and that meant everyone.

I'd start with Genevieve.

By the time the final bell rang, I knew just what I'd do. I'd storm down to the fair, bust into her trailer, and steal every memory *she* held dear. Teach her what it was like. And when she was reduced to a sobbing wreck, I'd laugh at her, turn around, and leave.

She deserved it.

My plan worked perfectly. Well, the storming and the barging part, at least. I elbowed my way past the line in front of Genevieve's trailer. That earned me some yells and crusty looks, but I didn't care. No one should be happy. What right did they have to it?

I slammed open Genevieve's door and stared down the old grandma who was sitting in front of her.

The old lady said something I ignored, but she stood and left in a huff. Genevieve stared at me, a slight smile on her face.

"What are you smiling at?" I snapped.

"My my my," she said. "Look who learned how to pilfer memories."

"You got a problem with that?"

She shrugged. "Not really. Went straight for the good stuff, did you? Where'd you manage to find that much hatred in less than a day?"

Enough with the talking. I was here to teach her a thing or two. Wipe that smile off her face. I stared at her and willed myself into her mind. There was the familiar *whooshing* sensation, and just as I was about to enter—

I slammed into a mental barrier. My mind went blank, and then I was stumbling backward, falling to the floor, stunned.

Genevieve stood in front of me, inhaling deeply, as if she

were smelling one of her favorite foods. She reached into a pocket in her dress and took out a small stoppered glass bottle. She removed the cork and concentrated. A glowing red light seeped into the bottle, seemingly from nowhere. One minute the bottle was empty; the next, there was light that grew brighter until it was as red as flame, and just as fierce.

She opened her eyes and grinned at the bottle. "Louis forgot all about how to do that, didn't he?"

I was still confused. What had happened to me? Why had I been in such a bad mood the entire day? Had I yelled at the bus driver? Yelled at the *principal*?

Genevieve continued. "It's a method that's frowned on in some circles. You can take a memory and store it somewhere other than yourself. Bottles make excellent receptacles. I don't think I've seen concentrated anger, frustration, and resentment in this high of a level. It'll be at least twenty doses, once I render it down."

My head felt like someone had used it for batting practice. "Doses?"

"At the Memoria Mensarius. Where else would I be selling all of what I steal? They're coming on Friday. I told you that, remember? In any case, I take out the details first. People buying anger want the pure emotion, not the memory of being angry at one person in particular, let alone all the petty reasons for the anger in the first place."

"So you admit it?" I asked. "That you're stealing memories?"

She shrugged. "Of course. Louis used to do the exact same thing, or did he fail to mention that? I'm not doing anything I wasn't taught how to do by him, so what makes me any different from you? I don't take anything that people haven't agreed to pay me. True, sometimes they don't fully understand what it is they're giving up, but *caveat emptor*. Buyer beware. And besides. You don't have anything to worry about. Louis made it so I can't steal from *you*. But you practically shoved this anger into my hands."

Genevieve went to a corner of the room and moved aside a curtain to reveal a big ornate cabinet covered in hand-carved decorations showing hunting scenes. Most of them violent. She tried to block my view, but I saw her reach behind the cabinet to grab a small silver key, which she then pretended to take out of another pocket on her dress. Once the cabinet was unlocked, she opened it to reveal shelves crammed tight with bottles identical to the one she'd just filled, all glowing with different colors and shades. Deep purples, bright yellows, faint greens. It looked like one of those crayon boxes with a rainbow of colors mixed together.

She caught me staring at the bottles, my mouth open in wonder. "Would you like to see them up close?"

I managed a nod and stood up, wobbling as I walked toward her. The colors from the jars cast a mottled sea of light onto the cabinet's walls and traced Genevieve's face in Technicolor. They triggered something in my mind. Some memory that I should have had, maybe, and didn't.

"This is just the latest haul from my autumn trip," she said. "That's why there's so much green and blue. Memories of the outside. Camping. Working in the fields. Hiking. It's what I come to Maine for. You'd be surprised how much some people are willing to pay for them in the city. Businessmen who haven't had a break in years, suddenly feeling like they just got back from a month-long vacation in the woods?"

She picked up one bottle and stared at the dark green inside it, like an emerald fresh from a mine. Genevieve went on, almost talking to herself. "And the best thing is that the people up here don't even really want memories in exchange. They've got so many of their own. What's one more camping trip? One more day in the garden? They don't want to actually own any other memories. They just want to spectate, like your sister. All I need to do is invest in crafting a few top-tier experiences and then rent them out, over and over. The other merchants on the Mensarius don't like to come to these sorts of places. Too focused on easier scores, I suppose. I practically have to bribe them just to show up, but they come when

135

I ask. You could meet them on Friday if you'd like."

"What are those?" I asked, pointing to a few that were tans and browns.

Genevieve set down the green bottle and picked up a beige one. "Skills. Crafts. Instruments. I don't take all of a skill from a person, of course. Not unless they insist. But if someone's been practicing a craft for decades, a year or two doesn't do much damage to them, and other people would love to have that sort of a head start on picking up a hobby. I could show you. Is there something you wish you could do better?"

Was she crazy? I wasn't going to chat with this woman like we were sharing a cup of cocoa around a fire. "What do you mean?" I asked, stalling the decision.

"Just what I said. Is there a skill you've always wanted? I'll give you one for free. As an example."

I hesitated still. Was this safe? But those bottles. Why couldn't I remember anything about them? "A skill?" I asked again.

"Anything you'd like," she said.

A skill. And I was supposed to go along with this. I put my hand in my pocket, feeling my Swiss army knife and thinking about the wood-carving competition. "Wood carving," I said.

Genevieve smiled and nodded, searching through the bottles for a moment before she found one: a dark rich brown that looked like glowing chocolate. "It goes to the nearest person when it's opened, but you shouldn't use it in a strong breeze. It could get blown away. Just stand still."

She opened the bottle.

The glowing color took a moment to emerge, almost as if it were hesitating. When it did come out, it was in a slow stream, tendrils of brown smoke coiling and undulating in the air like a snake charmer's cobra.

It dodged right and left, then turned to face me. In a single fluid motion, the entire thing left the bottle and rushed at my face. I flinched, but it kept coming.

What followed was close to what had happened with Louis the day before. Except instead of the knowledge of how to take memories, this was all about carving. How to hold the knife. How to select the right piece of wood. How to work with the grain and take what the wood could give you. How to keep the blade sharp and avoid getting your thumb sliced open.

All of that, all at once. One moment I was a kid who dreamed of being able to carve more than a misshapen horse, and the next I could craft an entire chess set. I wasn't a professional or anything, but I definitely wasn't an amateur.

"How's that?" Genevieve asked.

It was awesome. It was what I had dreamed about being able to do for years, and now I could do it. But I didn't want to let on I'd enjoyed it that much. "Interesting," was all I said.

She smiled and leaned back against the edge of her table. "That's one way to put it. And that's just two years of practice. I could give you another fifty right here on the spot. Turn you into a master. But, of course, it would cost you more than your father makes in a year. That skill I just gave you for free would normally run in the thousands of dollars."

"Why did you?" I asked, frowning.

"I like you. You remind me of myself."

No way. I would never steal the memory of one twin from another. I wasn't evil like that. I tried not to think about what I had done to my parents last night. That had been different.

Hadn't it?

She took out a pen and made some notations on the red bottle she'd taken from my memories—my parents' anger—then placed it on a shelf and closed the doors. "Don't think about getting in there," she said. "I lock it, and there are traps in case anyone tries to get inventive."

"What happened to Louis?" I asked out of the blue. "I saw a green light come out of a bottle like this, right before he died. Did you do that?"

Genevieve raised her eyebrows. "A green light? He might have been fiddling with things he didn't understand. The man was old and senile, after all, but he was a fantastic teacher, in his own way . . ." She trailed off again in thought.

"He taught you?" I asked. Someone knocked on the trailer door.

Genevieve ignored the noise. "I was his last apprentice. He taught me the basics, and I moved on from there. I'm imagining he gave you his knowledge when he died?"

I nodded, not sure if there was a reason to hide it. "How did you know?"

"You get used to the signs to look for when someone's monkeyed around with memories. I heard Louis had died, and then I talked with a policeman who was missing a few memories from after the death. Since Memory Thieves don't usually make it to backwater towns in Maine, I figured he must have passed on the skill before he died. Then you show up here brimming with stolen anger. It wasn't hard to put the pieces together."

"Stolen anger?" I asked.

She glanced back at the cabinet. "Parents fight? I've seen plenty of that. Most people just try to get rid of their memory of the fights. You're the first boy I've met who tried to remove the *parents'* memory of the fights. What were you thinking? You can't take thirty years of that kind of level of memories and just expect to ignore it."

"But Louis—I mean his memories—said you could—"

"Repress them," Genevieve said, sitting down on the table. "Sure. But memories are like weights. The stronger you are, the more you can handle. You tried to lift about two tons of memories using a body that's only ever handled a hundred pounds. And anger's a beast to handle. I don't think I would have trusted myself with that much longer than a minute or two at most."

"Then how did you steal the memories back?" I asked. "I thought you said—"

"Louis made it so I couldn't steal from you?" Genevieve scratched the back of her head idly as she continued. "Your mind was rejecting those memories. It couldn't handle so much at once of such a strong emotion, so it was trying to get rid of them any way it could, and I happen to know a thing or two about how to handle situations like that. And it's a good thing I came along. Any longer, and you would have started doing really foolish things. Not to mention the fact that the memories would have warped you."

I narrowed my eyes. "Why are you being nice to me?"

She laughed. "I'm not a monster, Benji. I'm a business-woman sitting on top of a tremendous opportunity." She got up and went to a window, pulling aside the curtain to look out. "Those people you see there? They have needs. Memories they don't want anymore. Memories they wish they had. I buy or exchange or sell. What's so monstrous about that?"

"You cheat them," I said. "Kelly wouldn't have chosen to become what she is now."

Genevieve let the curtain drop and shook her head. "Wouldn't she? I didn't change her personality. You can't steal that. I just took away some of her memories. What she chose to do after she'd been paid for those memories . . . that was up to her. What did your parents do after you took their angry memories? Stay around and hug you?"

I didn't answer.

She sighed. "Memories are strange things. You think they're only loosely tied to identity, but in many ways, we're all their slaves. We make new decisions based on the memories of decisions we made yesterday or last year. Take out a memory here or there, and there's no way of knowing what's going to unravel."

"I need to go," I said, turning to leave.

"Come with me," Genevieve said, standing in front of me with her arms folded. "I could use your help if I want my business to take off. Let me bring you to the next level. You'll love it. Travel the country. See new things. Big things. Talk to important people. Learn about the world."

I didn't know what to say.

She kept going. "I'll make you a full-fledged partner. You'll have your pick of any memory you want. Free. Did you know I could win the Olympics in four different disciplines? Archery. Judo. Equestrian. Fencing. Anything's possible if you have the right memories, and you can get them all at the Memoria Mensarius."

Genevieve could sense I still wasn't sold. "But then again, maybe you don't want to be a Memory Thief. You didn't ask for it. I could understand that, so I'll make you a second offer. I'll sell you Kelly's memories in exchange for the memories Louis gave you yesterday. I'll even throw in your parents' memories, too. Everything can go back to the way it was."

I wanted to jump at the opportunity. Everything back to how it was? That would be perfect. I let go of the doorknob and turned to face Genevieve full on. I stared at her. At her short hair. Her open expression. Could it really be this simple?

"Can I think about it?" I needed to get her to let me leave.

"Of course," Genevieve said. "But hurry. The longer memories are bottled outside a mind library, the fuzzier they become. I'll have to render them soon, or they'll be useless. In the end, I don't sell specific memories. I sell emotions and experience. Soon those memories might not be salvageable, and I won't be able to return them. And if you want to come with me . . . Well, the fair is over at the end of the week. So don't dawdle."

I hesitated one more time, then nodded and left the trailer.

CHAPTER

11

SHOE POLISH

It was only once I was out in the fresh air again, with my mind clear from all those heavy, angry memories from my parents, that I realized just what I'd done.

I'd taken a huge chunk of my parents' identities, and they'd ended up in Genevieve's hands. My parents had disappeared. The whole idea had been to borrow the memories for a bit and see what sort of an effect that had. Instead, I'd permanently removed them.

Not only that, but it had distracted me from helping Kelly. Instead of just having my twin's memories, now Genevieve had my whole family's. Whose side was I on, anyway?

I froze.

Kelly.

I thrust my hand into my pocket. Sure enough, there were two sets of keys there: mine and Kelly's.

She was locked out of the house. Yes, she'd been mean to me the last two days, but that wasn't her fault. What kind of a failure of a brother was I? I'd been so angry. So upset with everything. She would have gotten on the afternoon bus and been stranded. Were Mom and Dad even home by the time she got there? Did she remember where we hid the spare key, or had Genevieve taken that memory, too?

I rushed to a pay phone, digging in my pockets for change. My parents had always insisted we carry quarters for emergencies. Too cheap to buy Kelly and me cell phones, or too worried about what we'd do with them. I punched the numbers and hoped Kelly would answer. Even a Kelly who had no clue who I was. It went to voice mail after the fourth ring, and my level of panic went up a few more notches. What if she was still outside? What if she completely gave up on her family? What if—

I ran to the north exit, not sure of how I would get home. We didn't live in the boonies, but this was rural Maine. It would be at least a forty-five-minute walk.

It took thirty-five minutes to run as fast as I could. I wished I were in better shape.

By the time I got home, I was out of breath, sweaty from head to toe, and there were five big blisters spread between my two feet. Thank goodness I'd been in too big of a rush to bring my backpack to the fair when I left school. It was still in my locker.

No sign of the car. The front door was locked. I'd been half hoping (half dreading) I'd find Kelly sitting on the front porch, crying. Or maybe hanging out with Sam. I fumbled in my pocket for my keys, but while I was still trying to put my key in the lock, the door opened.

Kelly stood there, already in her pajamas, frowning at me. "Are you really my twin?"

I rushed forward and gave her a huge hug. She tried to squirm away. "Let me go!"

"I'm sorry I wasn't here," I said.

"Like I care. But I've been looking at some of these family albums in the house. Either Mom and Dad went all out on this prank, or you're my twin."

"How did you get in?" I asked, pushing back from her and examining her for damage. A large black spot the size of a nickel obstructed half the white of her right eye, and her left eye had three separate spots in a triangle around her pupil. It had been one thing to see the spots on strangers. Seeing them on Kelly made my knees feel wobbly.

Would Genevieve have set things up so I couldn't get into

Kelly's mind? It felt like debating whether or not to run into a brick wall that might or might not be a hologram. If it had been anyone other than Kelly, I would have had to think about it a lot longer.

For my twin, I just hesitated a moment before diving in.

There was the whirl of color and the *swooshing* sensation, but nothing like a brick wall. And then I wasn't worrying anymore: I was already in her mind.

Kelly's library was an arcade. A big one, with rows upon rows of the stand-up machines arranged in a big warehouse room. It was lit with overhead floodlights, but a third of them were turned off, and a second third were flickering, giving the room a strobelike effect that made me sick to my stomach.

The exact sort of place where you'd expect to get ambushed by the Whispers.

I licked my lips, trying to fight off the butterflies and keep my mind occupied elsewhere. Whatever Genevieve had done in here, it hadn't been pretty, and Kelly hadn't been ready for it. I clenched my fist, fuming about how Genevieve had tried to tell me Kelly had wanted this. Every memory I had from Louis told me this should never happen.

Even as a part of me wondered what condition Mom's and Dad's memories would be in at the moment.

I stepped over to an arcade terminal (Super Street Fighter), focused on "memories of my twin," and pressed the "Start" button. The screen flashed for a moment, then made a punching sound and displayed an "Error: File Not Found" message.

What else had I expected? I wasn't going to be able to just give Kelly all of my memories, but I had an idea how I could help a little.

It started with getting out of her mind quickly. And not just because I might or might not have heard something whispering in the far corner of the room, echoing from the darkness.

"Spare key?" Kelly said, and it took me a moment to remember I'd asked her how she got inside. "Duh." She turned around and walked into the house, oblivious to the fact that I'd just been in her memory library. I followed.

Still no sign of Mom and Dad, but at least Kelly was somewhat better. She was even talking to me. She settled into the couch in the living room and stared at me. "So. How is it I have a twin brother I can't remember?"

I swallowed and cleared my throat. "This is going to sound crazy, but someone went inside your head and stole all your memories of me. She's evil, and she has to be stopped, but you were going to help me stop her, and so she got in the way."

Kelly let me continue, not objecting, not questioning. I

147

told her about our parents arguing and about trying to come up with a way to avoid them getting divorced. About Louis dying and Genevieve showing up. About stealing Mom's and Dad's memories, and Sam becoming Kelly's boyfriend.

"You didn't even recognize me," I said. "That's what hurt the most."

But all she said was, "Memory Thieves? And one of them was mucking around in my head?"

I nodded, not sure what else to add. Could I blame her for not really being worried about how I'd felt?

Kelly started massaging her temples. "I . . . remember. Pieces. Playing with someone as a kid. Going on trips in the car. It's like . . . I can remember *around* you. Did we set fire to the kitchen curtains one time?"

"Twice, actually. Mom and Dad blamed me the first time, so you said we should do it again so you could prove it wasn't just me."

She scrunched her eyes closed. "And I let her take my memories of you?"

"I don't think you would have done that without being tricked."

"And Sam Hyde *isn't* my boyfriend?"

"No," I declared. "Definitely not."

She opened her eyes. "But he remembers me being his girl-friend, too."

"I told you. Genevieve can give memories. She's somehow worked out a way to fabricate them."

Kelly nodded, staring at the wall. "I—It just doesn't—"

She put a hand to her forehead, wincing in pain.

I rushed over to her side. "Let me help," I said.

"How? My head is killing."

"I know from Louis's memories that taking them from someone the way Genevieve did to you can do strange things. Your body freaks out. But maybe if I let you into my mind, and show you some of my memories of you, it'll help."

She stared at me. "You can do that?"

"Easy," I said.

Kelly thought for a moment, then nodded. "Anything's better than this."

"Good," I said. "Take my hand."

And just like that, I was in my memory library with stiff-as-a-board Kelly lying on the bed. I didn't know how long I had before the Whispers showed up, so I went straight to work, collecting some of my favorite memories of Kelly over the years: vacations to Disney World, summers at the beach, playing pranks on the neighbors, trick-or-treating, Christmas mornings. One by one, I fed them into the TV in the corner, playing them through and watching as they displayed.

For me, it wasn't like I was there again. I'm not sure how I managed it. Maybe some instinctive trick I couldn't verbalize.

Instead, I just kept watch over Kelly and the room.

Waiting for the Whispers.

Even knowing they'd arrive, I was still struck with a jolt of fear the first time I heard the voice.

"You don't belong here."

I looked around the room. No one was there. The TV was playing a scene of Kelly and me opening matching bikes on our birthday. *Stay focused, Benji,* I told myself. *Don't pay attention to them.*

The birthday scene ended, and I put on a memory from three months later, when Kelly and I had made a trip down the road on our bikes. The weather had been perfect, and we'd spent the afternoon lying next to a stream, throwing rocks into it from time to time when we got bored. It had become one of our favorite spots near our house.

"Your sister is going to die," the Whispers said. "There's nothing you can do to stop it. You're making it worse. You're helping Genevieve. You might as well—"

"Shut up," I said, but the moment the words left my mouth, I knew it had been a mistake. Acknowledging the Whispers was the first step to really listening to them. Doing what they told you to do.

Sure enough, they laughed in response. A low, raspy laugh, peppered with a string of eerie giggles. The sort of laugh a serial-killer clown might make, right before it took out a razor blade and sliced through your throat.

Keep your mind occupied, Benji.

The laughter continued through the next three memories, broken up now and then by growls and random hisses. Nothing physical, nothing loud. Just low-level, constant threats.

"Come to the bookshelf, Benjamin."

Wouldn't it be better for me to just go over there and confront it? Show the Whispers I was up to the challenge?

My feet were already walking to the corner before I realized what I was doing. Shaking my head, I went back to stand by the bed. I would just focus on not moving my feet. If I didn't move my feet, I couldn't do anything else the Whispers told me to. Simple. Easy.

"Genevieve will win," they said. "You can't even resist us. What hope do you have against her? Your sister will be lost forever. You will go mad. Think of the guilt. Knowing for the rest of your life that you failed. And all because—"

"I could beat you," I snapped, taking a step forward.

"Come to the bookshelf, then, and prove it."

I stomped over. I would show it. It wouldn't—

Then I realized I was doing it again. Stupid. I glanced at the corner, considering going over even now. It was all I could do to resist the urge. Hopefully, what I'd shown her would be enough to help, because if I stayed any longer, I might not get out of here and still be sane.

I left the room, taking Kelly with me.

Back in our living room, I took a deep breath, glad to be away from the Whispers.

Kelly sat there, her hand in mine, her eyes closed.

"Did that help?" I asked her at last.

She nodded once, but then fainted, slumping into the couch as her eyes rolled back into her head.

"Kelly? Kelly!" But she was out cold.

My gut told me this was to be expected, even as my emotions were in an uproar. Kelly needed rest, I reminded myself. Her mind had to somehow come to peace with the fact that she was missing a chunk of her experiences, and that some of the things she thought were true, weren't. What I'd shown her would help with that, but it would take time to get used to it.

I took another look at my sister, then stood and stepped away from her. I had to trust Louis's memories and hope it would all turn out.

Mom and Dad showed up around seven, breezing in with takeout Chinese for four. On the plus side, they'd remembered us at last. On the minus?

Their eyes were black as night.

My stomach sank the moment they walked in, as I was faced with the damage I'd caused. What had I been thinking? I should have been smart. Should have just trusted

Louis's memories and not complicated things more.

But I'd done what I'd done, and there was no going back until I could get those memories from Genevieve.

Mom and Dad didn't say anything about where they'd been or how they were sorry they'd disappeared. No questions about school or homework. And while they might have been all smiles and sunshine, trying to talk to them or appreciate the happy mood was impossible. I couldn't look at them without seeing those eyeballs, black and filmed over.

A reminder of how I'd failed them so quickly, and so easily.

My parents let Kelly just stay on the couch, asleep. I kept eyeing her, wondering if she was really okay. But my gut said to leave her be, and so I did.

I tried to turn to my parents for help. They were the grown-ups. They were supposed to be the ones to solve big problems like Genevieve. But they brushed off my questions at dinner. I tried Dad again when he was channel surfing later. "Dad?"

"What?"

"Do you think memories are important?"

He grunted, staring at that screen, oblivious to the fact that his eyes were both totally black.

I tried again. "If someone was in town stealing memories from other people, or trading for them, or something, and you could stop them or join them, what would you do?" Okay, so that was the worst description of my problem ever, but I'm not good at expressing things sometimes.

"That's nice," Dad said.

"No," I said. "You're not listening. I've got a problem here. Can you help me?"

He yawned and checked his watch. "Eight thirty. Mom and I are going to be late for the movie. Want to come?"

"No," I said. "I want help."

Dad stood up and left the room, like he hadn't even heard me.

That was the extent of the parental advice I got. So much for having help deciding what to do.

I checked myself. That wasn't fair. They'd been supportive of me until I messed with their memories. I had known better. Sure, they'd been mad at me, but you didn't get mad at people unless you cared about them. I'd just swiped any time they'd been angry at each other. How many times had those reasons for anger been tied to me or Kelly? I hadn't even thought to check. If I'd left them alone, then maybe they'd be able to help me now.

That night, I lay in bed staring at the ceiling and tried to get to sleep, but I couldn't stop worrying. I'd moved Kelly up to her room. It had felt wrong to leave her on the couch, and although she'd woken up enough to half walk herself up the stairs, as soon as I'd put her in her bed, she'd rolled over and gone back to dreamland without so much as a mumbled thank-you.

Who knew how long she'd be that way, and what she'd be like when she finally came to?

Meanwhile, Genevieve was wreaking havoc in my town, and no one had any idea what she was doing but me. For anyone else, she could just dive into their memories and steal anything she didn't want them to have.

It wasn't right.

I sat up in my bed. I knew what I had to do, even if it scared me. Genevieve could make all the claims she wanted about helping people and providing a good service, but she hadn't helped Kelly, and stealing memories hadn't helped my parents.

She had offered to give me back the memories I'd stolen if I'd give her the memories from Louis. But if I did that, she'd just sell them to someone else, and who knew what that person would use them for. I couldn't give the memories back, or trade for them, but I *needed* to get the ones I'd stolen.

What if I waited and went to see her again tomorrow? I could maybe steal some money from my parents and . . .

That was a bad idea. Stealing from my parents was wrong.

Stealing from Genevieve, on the other hand . . .

The plan hit me all at once, fully formed. I could convince Genevieve to give me the memories. Trick her the same way she'd tricked Louis. I could break into her trailer tonight, grab a bunch of memories she had stored there, and use them as a bargaining tool. I wouldn't give them back to her unless she gave everything back to me. The whole town, starting with Kelly and my parents. All the memories back, or I'd ruin everything for her. It wasn't stealing if you were taking back what was stolen to begin with, right?

It was blackmail. Nice and simple.

I had to be careful, and that meant preparation. A flashlight to see my way around and read the labels on all those bottles. A warmer jacket for the long walk back to town. Cargo pants with lots of extra pockets to store things, though once I had them on, the only thing that really made sense to take was my Swiss army knife. It fit perfectly into a zippered pocket down on my left pant leg. I stuffed my bed with pillows to make it look like it was still occupied. The last thing I needed was for my parents to have a bout of responsibility hit them and discover I was missing.

I felt like a monster, leaving Kelly alone and helpless in the house. And I couldn't help but notice the parallels to what she'd done just a few nights ago: leaving me to go at night and confront Genevieve. That had ended in disaster. I could only hope this went better. It was our only chance.

In case Kelly woke up—and hoping against hope that she might actually remember something about me when she did—I wrote a letter:

Kelly,
I've gone to the fair to get your memories back. DO NOT COME AFTER ME. I'll see you in the morning, and everything's going to be okay. I promise.
                                                                    —Benji

Not my best composition, but it should keep her calm until I was back. Hopefully, I'd be able to remove the letter without her ever knowing it was there.

At 10:30, I left.

There's an old railway bed that leads into town, passing not too far from my house. The county converted it to a walking path and cross-country ski trail a decade or two ago. It's not a direct route—you have to go out of your way to get onto it, which makes the walk longer—but I wanted to go unseen. It wasn't lit at night, and no one used it after seven or so. Walking on the main road would be too obvious and dangerous. No sidewalks. It was one thing to jog it during the day. At night? I'd probably get hit by a car that didn't see me. There wasn't a ton of traffic this late, but still enough to be worried about.

So the railway bed it was.

I'd dressed all in black for the occasion, even rooting around in my dad's closet for some of his shoe polish to make my face dark. I inspected myself in the mirror, pleased with the results. People would have a hard time seeing me, that was for sure. Especially if I closed my eyes. I'd read that was what usually gave people away at night—the whites of their eyes, and the reflection they made in the dark. I wouldn't make that mistake.

I had needed to use my dad's camping backpack, since mine was still at school. His smelled like campfire and bug spray, even though it had been at least two years since he'd used it. Loaded with my flashlight, some water, and a couple of snacks, it didn't weigh too much.

The neighborhood was empty. There were few houses on our street, with big gaps of forest or hay fields in between. I walked on the side of the road, ducking into the underbrush on the two occasions a car drove by. When your face is painted black and you're dressed in dark colors, it's hard to claim you were just out for a midnight stroll. Plus, it made me feel kind of cool, like I was an elite soldier on a secret mission.

And really, wasn't I? I had an ability no one else had. Hardly anyone else, at least. I was going to break into a guarded facility and escape with top-secret information. It didn't get more elite than that.

To get to the railway bed, I had to cross one of the big roads that led into town. This late, even that only had a handful of cars on it. I waited for a good break, then sprinted across.

It was a straight shot from there on out.

The closer I got to the fairgrounds, the more nervous I became. At first I could focus on the excitement, but then I started thinking about all the ways this could go wrong. The fair had to have guards, didn't it? Usually, in movies and books, people would throw a rock in another direction. The guards would go to where the rock had been thrown, and you could waltz in once they were gone. Did that work in real life?

It didn't matter, though. Right? Because I could let the guards catch me and then steal their memories of me once I was caught. Unless they shot first and asked questions later.

I didn't *think* the fair would have armed guards, but you never knew. And once I was in the fairgrounds, how would I get inside Genevieve's trailer? And what was that booby trap she'd been talking about when she warned me not to try?

None of that mattered, I decided, clenching my jaw and straightening my back. My footsteps sounded resolute on the dirt path. Forceful. I was the only one who had a chance of dealing with this problem. The police would never believe this story. And if the police were out, you could bet the army wasn't coming. Maybe I could contact the FBI. Didn't they have people who dealt with this stuff? But even if they did, Washington was a long way away. Genevieve said those memories would decay with time.

I made it to the fairgrounds with little incident. And there *were* guards. Well, *a* guard. I waited for fifteen minutes. The night watchman came by once. The gate was locked, and a chain-link fence surrounded the whole area. Then again, every boy half my age knew chain link was made to be climbed over. Yes, it made a ruckus when you did it—rattling to be heard across the whole fairgrounds. And yes, it made the watchman come investigate, but a quick dive into his memories (which took the form of a public library, strangely enough) erased that problem. I let him go on his merry way with no memories of me.

From there, it was just a matter of staying in the shadows until I was at Genevieve's trailer.

I studied it. What if she was inside waiting for me? This might be a trap, and if it was, I didn't want to fall for it. I scrounged around for a rock and threw it through one of the windows, which shattered in a tinkling of glass.

I waited.

No one came. Not even the guard who had heard me before. The minutes passed. I checked my watch again.

Fifteen minutes gone. I'd already done the breaking. It was time for entering.

I got out of my crouch and rushed over to the broken window, clearing out the shards of glass with my Swiss army knife, which I tucked back into my zippered cargo-pant pocket once I was done. The window was high off the ground; I'd had to stand on my tiptoes to get the other glass out. I wasn't sure all the shards were gone, so I wrapped my coat around my hands and used that to grip the frame.

For a few seconds, I wasn't sure if I was going to be able to lift myself up and in. My feet scrabbled at the side of the trailer, straining to get some traction. And just when I was going to give up and try something else, I managed to get a good grip and vault in through the window. Or stumble in, at least.

I landed in a sprawl on the floor, convinced Genevieve was waiting for me after all. Any moment, she'd spring from the darkness and—I opened my eyes. No one was there. The only illumination came in through the broken window, casting a puddle of light where I lay but leaving the rest of the room in shadowed outlines.

Stupid, Benji. Overreacting again. I took the flashlight out and switched it on, surprised by how bright it was. I placed my hand over the front of it, shielding some of the light. No sense calling more attention to myself than necessary.

The cabinet looked different in the dark. Without

Genevieve peering over my shoulder, I could study it more carefully. And now that I had those few years of wood-carving practice she gave me, I had an even better idea just how hard it would be to make a piece of art like this. One wrong move of the blade and that antler on the stag that was getting its throat slit would be ruined. The hounds tearing apart the fox were in exact proportion right down to the claws on their feet. These carvings came alive at night. It must have been the way my flashlight moved over them. It was as if you could see each scene happening in real time.

Creepy. A sense only heightened by seeing the glowing memories' light bursting through the crack between the doors. I held my hand up against it, watching the light cast mottled waves on my skin.

When I felt around at the back of the cabinet for where I'd seen the key, I had another setback.

It wasn't there.

Genevieve must have known I'd seen where she kept it, and so she'd taken it.

I looked at the lock, hoping it would be one of those cheap ones like they had on suitcases. I'd brought some paper clips, and I could pick those pretty easily. You just bent the paper clip, stuck it in, and moved it around some until it clicked.

This was a normal lock made for a real key.

Paper clips weren't going to cut it.

I sighed and took out the paper clips anyway. It wasn't even midnight yet. I had plenty of time to pick the lock before morning. But the paper clips I'd brought were too thick. They wouldn't even go partway into the lock. What was I going to—

My flashlight shone into the crack between the doors of the cabinet, hitting the bottles and nothing else. Meaning no latch—the door wasn't locked?

I set the flashlight down and pulled gently on the door, just enough to test the lock. I had been right. It was open.

Why would Genevieve leave the cabinet unlocked? She'd said it was booby-trapped, but didn't it make sense to lock it, too? I would never leave my treasures unlocked.

Either the booby trap was so good that locks didn't matter, or this whole situation was a trap. She *wanted* someone to come and try to open her cabinet.

It's not often you have to make a bad decision, knowing ahead of time it's a bad decision. Well, there were plenty of times on multiple-choice tests where I had no idea what the answer was, so I just picked one of the five, fairly confident I was picking the wrong one.

This was like that, except with my family members' lives in the balance. But really, what choice was there? I needed those memories. They were in that cabinet. I had to get into it.

I took a breath, held it, and opened the door.

CHAPTER

12

DEPRESSION

A bottle teetered just inside the cabinet, balanced to fall out when the door opened. I tried to catch it, but it fell to the floor and shattered, releasing a glowing black ooze into the air. I had no idea what emotion that was, but I didn't want to get it.

I stumbled back, scrabbling away on all fours, but the ooze dove at me. I rolled to my right, bumping into the table, and the ooze sailed wide. Maybe I could escape. Since the ooze had missed me, had it gone to find someone else? I turned to see it hovering in the air, pulsating and quivering like a swarm of bees.

It twitched to the left, then bobbed up and down. I scrambled backward until I was pressed up against the wall. Was it lethal? Did Genevieve have some horrific memory that could scare you to death?

My pulse pounded in my head.

The ooze surged forward, and now there was no way to avoid it. I had an instant to put my hands up to protect my face, but it whipped around them without a pause. It was cold and damp as it passed my hands, like a drowned body. And then that cold was burrowing into my eyes and nose and mouth, and I couldn't even scream.

I blinked, staring in front of me. I was sitting on the floor in the trailer. It was dark out, but I didn't mind the dark. The dark fit my mood. Moving was pointless, so I just sat there, lost in thought.

After all, I was a complete failure. Doing anything other than sitting made no sense. Why had I bothered trying? Everything had gone wrong since I came to the fair. My parents hated each other. My twin couldn't stand me. No one liked me at school. Why had I thought for a moment that I might be able to fix anything?

A hint of movement caught my eye, and I looked over to see a carpenter ant crawling its way across the fake-wood floor. The size of the room dwarfed it, a small creature trying to go from one point to another through a huge cavernous expanse, full of darkness, with just a hint of moonlight to light its way. At any moment, it could get stepped on or blown off course, and even if it made it wherever it was going, it would just have to turn around and go back to get home. A pointless journey, and for what? A bread crumb?

How was I any different from that ant?

Being here was a mistake. But going home didn't feel like a good idea, either. Better to sit here and wait for Genevieve to show up and kill me. I'd be better off. No way to make mistakes anymore. No one could be mad at me. Everything would be better if I didn't exist.

At the back of my head, a small voice said something about repressing memories.

That voice didn't know what it was talking about. These *were* my memories. My memories of failure and incompetence. I had no friends. Even Kelly had proved she didn't really like me. She had a chance to ditch me, and she took it. My parents hated me. I'd yelled at everyone at school today. I'd been to the principal's office. I was doomed to a life of crime.

Repress this memory. This isn't you. It's from that black ooze.

I ignored the thought. Easier to just sit there. And stare.

Seconds ticked by. They turned into minutes. The voice in the back of my head kept trying to break through, but I had no desire to listen to it. It was easier to just think about my failures. How everything had gone wrong.

But what about Kelly?

That thought broke through where the others had failed. I'd written her that note, after all. Promising I'd be back. What would she do if I wasn't home? She'd come find me, and when she did, Genevieve would finish picking her memories over.

It didn't matter.

If I tried to do anything, I'd only fail. Again. Kelly was a lost cause no matter what.

But if you don't try to help her, how will you live with yourself?

That was a question I didn't have an answer to. Trying was only going to go wrong, but maybe not trying at all would be even worse. Could I even snap out of this whatever-it-was Genevieve had hit me with? What was it exactly?

And then something clicked in my head. My back was straightening. My mind was able to look at the memories Genevieve had left for me, and now they were something that could be picked apart. Analyzed. I felt like a scientist who had caught the disease he was studying, except I knew how to treat it. How to isolate that disease and scrutinize it until I knew how to cure it.

It was a complex mixture of memories, culled from many

people over the years. And each person it had invaded had made it stronger. Genevieve had been using this trick for years. I sensed others it had destroyed. A woman who'd come looking for her husband and found this cabinet instead. A grandfather who'd sold his ailing wife's memories but then regretted it. If their memories were still encased in this trap, it made me wonder what had happened to the rest of them. Their happier memories. Had Genevieve taken those, too?

As soon as I started worrying about the other people in that trap, my own depression became easier to handle. It was no longer mine. I could repress it. And with a surge of emotion, I came back to myself. I was Benji. I wasn't a failure. I was a boy in a bad situation, and I was making the best of it.

And I needed to go save my sister once and for all. Find a way to fix her.

But I wasn't going anywhere if Genevieve caught me. I had to hightail it out of here.

I opened my bag and loaded it with bottles. No time to worry which ones were which. I'd need as much leverage as I could get. Genevieve had to see that it would be worth more to trade with me than to—

The door opened, and the light from the memories traced the outline of Genevieve's pretty face.

My stomach dropped like a rock, but I had the presence of mind to shove two bottles of memories into my back pockets while she was looking outside, maybe making sure no one was around. No clue what was in the bottles, but better to have them than to not.

"Well," she said. "Who'd have thought I'd find you here at this hour?" She didn't sound surprised. She was back in her jeans and tight T-shirt. Her tattoos looked even more fearsome in the dim light. Skeletons and rotting flesh and burning bodies and blood blood blood. "The depression didn't quite work on you, did it?" she said, then shrugged. "I'd thought the memories from the old coot might give you an out there. Looking for something? It's hard to find what isn't there."

She reached into her back pockets and took out two bottles. I didn't need to read them to know they were the ones I was looking for.

I stood, knocking some of the other bottles over. They clanked together and rolled around on the floor.

"Careful," Genevieve snapped. "You break anything, and I'll make you pay extra."

"I need those," I said, pointing at the bottles she held.

"Of course you do. And let me tell you how you're going to get them. You're going to open your mind to me and let me take Louis's memories. I'll also take back the depression trap you sprang, thank you very much, and you'll thank me for it. You've beaten it for now, but something that powerful is hard to swallow for too long before it twists you—something you discovered with your parents' memories, yes? Once I have those memories in hand, you can have these back, and we'll all go on our merry way. Deal?"

"How do I know I can trust you?" I asked.

"Let me give you the alternative. You've broken into my trailer. I could call the guards and try to have you arrested, but that would just end with you and me stealing the guards' memories until the cows come home. So instead, I'll lock you up in a secret room underneath this trailer. I won't let you out until you agree to give me those memories. If anyone comes looking for you, I'll take their memories of you until no one in this pisspot of a town even knows you exist. So isn't the choice easier? Just open up your mind to me, and this will all be over."

I watched her eyes closely. "Promise me you'll leave me the rest of my memories, and that everything will be like it was before." I'd read a book that said you could tell when a person was lying by watching which way their eyes went when they spoke.

She looked straight back at me. "I promise."

So much for watching which way her eyes went. She seemed sincere. And what chance did I have at a better option? There was nothing else I could do.

I was about to say yes. I really thought I was going to. But somehow, my mouth said no instead. And once that "no" was out, I knew it had been the right choice.

Genevieve's lips pressed together in a thin line, and she grabbed my arm and shook me. "Listen, you brat. You're giving me those memories. Right now."

I tried to scramble away from her—wrench my arm free and make a break for the door. But Genevieve hadn't been kidding when she'd told me she could win a gold medal in judo. With a simple sidestep and twist of her hand, I was on the floor with my wrist held far up behind my back. My eyes watered in pain, and I screamed out.

Genevieve hit me over the head hard enough for me to black out.

I came to when she threw some water on my face, opening my eyes to see she had revealed a trapdoor in the floor, a gaping pit leading down to darkness.

"Last chance," Genevieve said.

I had to blink a few times to clear my head. My hands were tied behind my body, tight enough that the cord bit into my skin. She'd bound my legs, too. I thought about the bottles in my back pockets. The Swiss army knife in my secret pocket. I'd figure a way out of this. Somehow. "Never," I said, because it sounded like the thing to say in a situation like this.

"Let's see what you think in twelve hours or so. You have until sunset. Or else."

Genevieve shoved me down. I fell seven or eight feet to a dirt floor with a *thump*, the wind exploding from my lungs. And then she slammed the trapdoor shut above me, leaving me in darkness.

CHAPTER

13

SILENCE

I struggled against my bindings with no luck. I hadn't slept, and I couldn't move. It was cold down in that hole, and pitch-black. After who knew how long, I fell asleep.

Sunlight shone through the boards lining the walls above me when I woke up. I looked around in the dim light. I was in an eight-foot pit beneath Genevieve's trailer. Now I knew what that man with the wheelbarrow and dirt had been up to, way back when I first came here. The floor and walls were rocky earth until about five feet up, at which point rough pine boards boxed in the area between the ground and the trailer.

There were gaps in the boards, sometimes as wide as a centimeter or two. If I stood on my toes and pressed my eyes against one of the gaps, I could see outside to the fairgrounds. Latticework surrounded the outside edge of the area beneath the trailer. There was no way people walking by would see me unless they crouched next to the trailer and peered in. Even then, they'd just be able to see there was some kind of enclosure down here.

Still, I could already hear the dull roar of a crowd forming.

Screaming was going to do me no good. Fairs aren't the quietest of places, and those boards were pretty thick. I had about as much chance of being heard as I would have in the middle of a rock concert. If I was going to get out of this, I was going to have to do it on my own. Genevieve clearly thought I'd be helpless.

It was up to me to prove her wrong.

My hands were tingling where the cords cut into my wrists. My Swiss army knife was in my zippered pocket, but that was on the front left side of my pants. No matter how I contorted, I couldn't reach it. In movies and books, you could just switch your arms out from behind your back by slipping them over your legs, but either the movies and books lied, or my arms and legs didn't work that way. Whenever I tried, my shoulders flared up in agony, and the bindings on my wrists felt even worse. The cords had started to cut into my wrists: I could feel blood dripping down my hands onto the dirt.

But there was no way I was going to give up. Not with my whole family depending on me, not to mention the whole town. I was covered in a mixture of blood, sweat, and mud. The pit stunk, and it hadn't helped that I'd had no place to go to the bathroom. I'd set off yesterday evening with one hope: use Genevieve's stolen memories as leverage to get her to give my family their memories back. It had all gone terribly wrong.

Still, there had to be a way out of this. I just had to find the right approach.

The door to Genevieve's trailer opened with a squeak, and I looked up. Her trailer floor had cracks in it, allowing me to catch a glimpse of what was going on up there. Enough to get an idea, at least. I saw her stride into the room, now in a sweeping midnight-blue dress that was little more than a shadowed outline to me. I yelled and hollered and made an idiot of myself, not because I thought she'd reconsider, but because I wanted her to be certain there was no way I was getting out of that pit.

Fifteen minutes later, the first customer walked in.

Another squeak of the door. Some muffled conversation that I could barely make out. It was a man. Big tree-trunk arms, thick neck.

I screamed again. "Help! I'm locked down here! Someone help me, please!" My voice echoed in my ears, but just as I'd expected, the ground and the thick wooden planks swallowed the sound.

There wasn't even a pause in the conversation above me. Genevieve must have been pretty confident when she stuffed me down here. Had she done something like this before? And all this was supposed to change my mind somehow? Make me more willing to trust her?

If I was quiet, I could make out a few words of what was being said above me. Enough to get an idea of what was going on. The man had memories of someone. His daughter? Brother? But that person was dead, and he didn't want to remember them. Was he mad at them? Did he miss them too much?

The man wanted to sell those memories for cash. Genevieve obliged. Things went very still upstairs for a full minute, and then she was seeing the man to the door.

I didn't think she'd paid him, but maybe I had missed something.

She didn't pay the next three people, either. I was watching for it, and I realized what was happening. She'd bargain with them and then take away their memory of what they'd agreed to. Genevieve was pawing through the memories of every person who came into her trailer, taking what she wanted and leaving what she didn't, and not paying a single cent for anything.

Memory Thief, indeed.

Part of me wondered at how powerful Genevieve seemed. If she had all this ability, why was she trawling the backwoods of Maine? Shouldn't she be in some position of power? Couldn't she have finagled her way into politics?

Questions with no answer for now.

In the back of my mind, I remembered the note I'd written to Kelly, telling her where I was and what I was doing. What would she do when she found it? She should do what I'd asked and stay away. Her memory was coming back some, and she'd be able to iron out what was wrong with my parents if I disappeared permanently. Anything was better than them coming back here and letting Genevieve at them again. On the other hand, if she decided to come anyway, maybe together we'd be able to . . .

Better not to think about that. No sense having false hope. They'd be safer if they stayed away.

The next person in was a mother and daughter. The daughter was screaming. She couldn't have been more than eight years old. The mom had a brash voice that carried through the floorboards with an almost magical ease. I wished my voice could do that.

"Shut up, you. I told you it doesn't hurt."

More screams. Some words from Genevieve.

The mother again. "No. Just the girl. She must have something in that head of hers worth money."

More screaming, even louder now. She wasn't yelling words, she was just shouting out syllables. And then the screams cut off. Silence, which was even more disturbing than the girl's screams had been.

Genevieve said something again. The mother answered, "No. I've heard about you. My sister lives over in Newport, and she said you were liable to give folks a raw deal. I'll be taking payment, but you won't be getting any memories from—"

The mom's voice cut off as she had her memories wiped, too. Served her right, but I worried about the little girl, who wasn't crying or sobbing or anything anymore. I could have sworn she was actually *humming*, though it was hard to be certain, what with the noises wafting in from outside and the floorboards in between us.

The mother and daughter left soon after.

Back to working on my bonds.

The cords only cut into my wrists more, reopening the wounds. What if I struggled too much and sliced through an artery? I scaled back my efforts, frustrated, even though I reminded myself to stay positive. Minutes went by, then an hour. The sun's rays traced their way across the dirt walls.

More people came above me. Some screamed. Some haggled. All left with empty pockets and empty memories.

I was staring dully out through one of the cracks between the boards lining my pit, up on my toes for the millionth time, taking another break.

And then I saw her.

Kelly.

And she'd brought my parents.

Who knew how she'd done it or why—when I'd last left her, she'd still been half convinced I wasn't her brother—but she had.

I called out as soon as I saw her. "No! Stay away! Don't come in here!" Because I knew Genevieve would steal the rest of their memories, just like she'd stolen everyone else's. The woman could claim she was providing a simple service, but it was all thieving and nothing more. Crime with a thin layer of respectability, since no one could remember a crime had been committed once it was over.

My family tromped up the stairs. I jumped up again, trying to get their attention. I hit my head against the walls. I whistled. I stomped. And for a moment, Kelly stopped. She looked from side to side.

"Kelly!" I screamed, louder than I'd ever yelled anything in my life. "Go away! It's not safe!"

She hesitated a moment more. Had she heard? Had my

voice cut through everything to get to her?

And then she went the rest of the way into the trailer.

They were above me now. Kelly spoke, her tone full of accusation, though I couldn't make out what she was saying. Genevieve's voice was lilting and soothing in response.

"No!" I cried out again. Tears were falling down my cheeks. "Go away!" I tried to scream, but it only came out as a hoarse croak.

It grew silent upstairs, and that silence stretched forever.

A few seconds later the door opened. Three sets of footsteps made their way down the stairs. Kelly paused once more. Her shoulders drooped.

And then my family left without another question, their memories of me undoubtedly stolen.

I was completely alone.

14

LYING HERO

Genevieve opened the trapdoor at her lunch break. She let down a rope ladder. I was on the floor on my back, covered in dried blood and dirt and the remnants of my shoe polish camouflage from last night. I hadn't had a thing to eat the entire morning. Nothing to drink. I was tired, hungry, and depressed. Positive thinking can only bring you so far.

And Genevieve knew it.

Should I put up a fight? Rush up against the ladder when she didn't expect it? I'd want to make sure she didn't find the bottles I'd stashed away in my back pockets, but maybe I'd be able to knock her out. I'd turn around and use my hands to fumble through her pockets, where I'd discover a knife of her own. I'd cut my bindings and scramble up the—

That was all a pipe dream. I didn't have it in me. Genevieve came down the ladder, carrying a Coleman lantern, and I lay there. The harsh light of the Coleman made my prison look even worse. Rough boards. Crude walls. She turned and smiled at me. "How are we feeling?"

I didn't say anything in response.

Genevieve nodded. "Throat sore? I thought I heard you a few times, and I applaud your effort. But what did you hope to accomplish?" She held out a bottle of water, and I drank as best I could as she poured it down my throat. The water felt glorious on my face. So cool and fresh.

But I still didn't say anything.

She continued. "Let's imagine the impossible happened. Someone heard you. They found you were a prisoner. I keep little holes like this wherever I go. It makes some things much easier. And every now and then, someone finds them. Finds one of my guests. Do you know what happens then? Nothing. So what if the authorities show up? Two minutes with me, and no one remembers anything. There's no use fighting it, Benji. Don't you see? So just give me those memories. I'll still honor my promise and return your family's memories."

I had to clear my throat three times before anything would come out. "I've seen how you keep your promises. No deal."

The pressure of the bottles in my back pockets was hard to forget. Would she find them? What would she do if she did? And even if I got out of my bonds, would they do any good?

"I thought you might say that." She reached into her pocket and took out a shining silver bottle. "This is the latest batch from your family. You took their anger? I took their happiness. Every last drop. Do you remember what it was like when you got hit with my depression trap? That's what your family is going through now. And you're the only person who can save them."

This wasn't happening. Who could be that cruel? I struggled against the bonds again, but it did no good. "And why should I trust you? You'll do the same thing to me you've done to everyone else. You're the most vile, despicable person I've ever met. You make serial killers look like Santa Claus."

She reached back as if she were about to slap me, then stopped and took a moment to regain her composure. "This is the end of my trip. I'm meeting up with the black market tonight. Fair season is over, and there's stuff to pack, inventory to take, and I can't be worrying about the brat in my basement. So here it is. Last chance. Give me the memories, or I'm selling these, and you'll never get them back."

I shook my head. "Never."

"Maybe you don't get it. I have other options." Genevieve thrust her hand into her pocket and took out a bottle of the deepest blue I'd ever seen. She waved it in front of my face. Even with just a glimpse of it, I wanted more. It was such a wonderful hue. So deep. So dark.

"Don't look too hard," Genevieve said. "This stuff will catch you. Trap you. I have to put it in a special bottle just to keep myself from getting ensnared. It's concentrated amnesia. Give it to a Memory Thief like you or me, and it doesn't just make us forget things. It evicts all the memories we have from our minds. Everything. If I give this to you, you'll be left with exactly what you came into this world with. You'll be a twitching, spasming, crying newborn in a body that happens to be twelve years old. You won't know how to talk or walk. You won't be toilet trained. You'll have to learn how to do all of that all over again, except this time your parents won't know who you are. They won't care who you are. You'll be shuffled off to some room in a state hospital. It will ruin your life completely."

She took a step back and folded her arms. "I know you think I'm a monster, but a real monster would just give this to you and not care about it. A real monster would have done it days ago. The abilities you have in that head are priceless. They would sell for enough to buy me my own private island. I'd never have to work another day in my life. Never have to go to these worthless towns again. What good are they doing you? They've ruined your life in less than a day. I'm going to get those memories, Benji. I'm going to the Mensarius tonight at eight, and they're all going to be in a little bottle. I'll stop by here once more on my way. When I do, you'll get only one chance to give me the memories. Otherwise, it's the amnesia. Don't make me be a monster."

Genevieve took the Coleman lantern and left.

At least she hadn't found the bottles.

I lay there on the ground, still bound, listening to my breath and thinking about what it would be like to be a newborn again. Genevieve was right. It would be horrible. Shouldn't I just give up? Give her the memories? But if I let her into my mind, there was no guarantee she'd just take those memories. Sure, she wouldn't leave me with nothing, but all the stuff I valued might be gone. I just couldn't bring myself to really trust Genevieve.

I'd tried the whole day to get free of those bonds. I'd twisted, writhed, contorted, and bent. Nothing had worked. But when the clock's ticking, and the threat is real enough, do you just sit there and wait for the end to come, like a cow gazing placidly at the bolt gun?

I don't.

I thrust my arms down as far as they would go, turning my wrists in an effort to get more space. I scrunched up my legs as close to my body as I could. But my legs weren't the problem. My butt was. My wrists were tied so tightly together that I couldn't slip them down under my bum. If I could just get my arm over the edge of my hip, then I'd be home free.

Well, as long as "home free" meant "stuck in a pit with no ladder or hope for escape."

But step one was definitely getting myself free of those bonds. I'd deal with the rest if I could only get that far.

It was getting hotter in the pit. But as I lay there, becoming more and more convinced there really was no hope, a memory popped into my head from two years ago: my dad, telling me how to solve math problems. I'd been working on homework for two hours, and I was struggling. Dad told me that sometimes people get so focused on solving a problem one certain way, they forget there are other options. Trying to break down a door, for example, when a window turns out to be unlocked. You get so focused on opening that door, you forget the only reason you want to open the door is so you can get outside.

Once you remember that you're breaking down a door *in order to get outside*, you can stop focusing on the door and start looking for other ways to get outside.

It hadn't helped with the math problems, but it might help me now.

What had I been trying so far? To get my wrists over my feet so they were in front of me. Why did I want to do that? So I could reach my pocket. Was there another way? The stuffiness down here made it hard to concentrate, and I took a few deep breaths to focus.

Another way.

My hands couldn't get to the Swiss army knife. Could the Swiss army knife get to my hands?

I lay down on my side and tilted my left leg—the one with the pocket that held my Swiss army knife—as far up as it would go, turning so my left hand was as close to it as it could stretch. I was still a foot short. Could I get the knife closer?

Taking my pants off would work. But when I tried that, I discovered my belt was buckled on too tight and didn't want to slip down my hips.

What if I tried to hike the pocket higher? I inched it up with my fingers, though they were turning numb, and fumbled at the fabric. But once the pants bunched up to a point, they couldn't get any higher. The knife was closer— three or four inches—but not close enough.

My hands were useless. So what else was there? Why was I doing what I was doing? To get the Swiss army knife. Why did I need that? To cut my bonds. Was there another way to do that? Was there something sharp I could rub up against? Nothing I'd come across during the day. Maybe I could have gnawed through the cords if I could get my teeth around to—

My teeth.

The thought hit me like a ton of dirt. I couldn't get my hands to my pocket. This whole time, it had all been about my hands. But I could get my teeth there, couldn't I?

I leaned forward and fumbled at my pants with my lips and tongue. They were covered in dirt, but by pinching the fabric with my teeth, I could maneuver it into a better position. I felt like an idiot. Why hadn't I thought of this sooner? If I'd only—

No. No "if onlys." I hadn't thought of this sooner, and that was what it was. I'd thought of it *now*, and maybe there was still time to do something.

It took some work to get the pocket in reach and open its zipper and get the Swiss army knife out, but in the end, the knife fell to the dirt floor with a light thud. I whirled and started feeling for the knife with my hands. From there, it went smoothly.

I got the blade open with more effort, twisted it around in my hands so that it was up against the bindings, only to discover they weren't made out of cord at all. They were zip ties. No wonder they'd been hurting me so much. I slowly began moving the blade back and forth. It wasn't razor sharp. I'd used it a lot. Would it be sharp enough to cut through the cord? Should I have sharpened it?

After five minutes of sawing at the plastic, my hands were tingling even more, and they needed a rest. I felt at where I'd been sawing. Sure enough, there was a tiny nick in the zip tie.

It was working. Just slowly.

It must have taken at least twenty minutes, but in the end, the ties popped free with a snap.

I gasped in relief and pain as my arms came forward for the first time in a day. I rolled my shoulders and wrists to get feeling and use into them again. My wrists were ragged and cut from the plastic, the skin bleeding. Ugly. When I had a chance, I'd need to patch them up.

One thing at a time.

I reached in my back pocket for the two memory bottles I'd managed to bring with me. They weren't labeled. One glowed green, and the other was a dark purple. Would they be able to help me out of here? My mind raced over the skills that would help: cat burglary, martial arts, hunting, trapping, or hiding. I could become a physics genius and use science to take Genevieve down, or maybe become an expert archer or sharpshooter. Even if it was just something tame, like detailed knowledge of the fairgrounds, that would still be useful. No matter what they were, they had to be somehow better than what I had now.

Only one way to find out.

I uncorked the green one first.

The green mist billowed out of the bottle, tendrils crawling over the top and stretching out into the air. I leaned over and breathed them in.

With a rush, ten years of experience washed over me.

Words like downward-facing dog, half cobra, lord of the dance, lying hero, crane, and bikram triangle. Body positions, breathing techniques, meditation styles. My breathing evened out some, and I had a much greater awareness of my body, all at once. Like I knew where my arms were and what my legs were doing, where before I only really thought of stuff like that when I was paying attention.

For a moment, I thought I'd scored the mother lode. This had to be advanced-level karate or kung fu. I'd be a fighting machine. Unstoppable.

Then the rest of the memories settled into place, and I realized I hadn't become a ninja.

I'd gotten ten years of yoga experience.

It didn't come with the flexibility needed to put it into practice, however. My mind knew how to do things my body wasn't capable of. I'd need to train to get the rest of myself up to speed with what I'd just learned.

In the meantime, knowing how to do a perfect greeting pose wasn't likely to win me any battles with Genevieve.

I fought back a sigh, focused my chakra, and tried to stay positive. The memories weren't like what I'd gotten from Louis or my parents. Genevieve must have done something to them to make them less . . . assertive. I didn't feel like they were going to overpower me (if yoga could be said to overpower anything). And I had to remember: I still had one bottle left.

Time for the purple.

Once again, the mist came out of the container, and once more I hesitated just a moment before breathing it in.

A flood of information came to me, filled with tiny figures and sprawling maps. Probabilities, tactics, newsgroup debates, strategies, and more. Titles like Twilight Struggle, Eldritch Horror, Dominion, War of the Ring, or Agricola. And while strategies and tactics seemed like a good thing at first, I soon realized they were all focused around every kind of board game you could think of.

There had to be twenty years' worth of board-gaming experience in that bottle.

So . . . if Genevieve wanted to bet everything on a game of Puerto Rico, I'd have a good chance of coming out on top.

My shoulders slumped, and I sank back against the wall of the pit. What were the odds that I'd get something that useless, not once but twice?

My gaming experience told me it was actually pretty good. There had been a bunch of memories in that cabinet, and they were all from around Livingston. It wasn't going to be ninja skills and tracking.

But I had to go forward. Had to do something. I knew what I had available to me now. Maybe I'd been unlucky, but I had my hands free now. I could come up with a plan.

If I didn't, life would never be the same.

CHAPTER

15

HUNTING

My wood-carving experience and Swiss army knife came in handy when it was time to get out of that pit. I didn't have to bother with digging through the dirt. I just spotted the weak points in the wood and whittled into them. My knife might not have been the sharpest one in the world, but it was more than a match for the lumber Genevieve had used down here. Much of it was already moldy and splintering to begin with.

As I carved, I debated what my next move should be. In a way, those board-gaming skills came in handy. I had more experience breaking a problem down and approaching it without getting too personally involved in the decision. Keep your nerves calm, and you were able to think better than a person who got flustered and impatient.

What did I need to do? What was my objective?

I had to get the memories back from Genevieve. If I was gone from this pit when she came down to see me (and I was *going* to be gone from this pit), what would she do next, logically?

Sell them.

She'd said there was the Memoria Mensarius coming through this evening. She would go there and sell what she could. You could tell a lot from a player by how they acted and spoke. Genevieve was a backstabber. She'd want to get even with me for escaping, so she'd be sure to sell my family's memories, even if she had to take a loss to do it.

Winning a game was much easier when you could guess what your opponent was going to do ahead of time. You just had to take that into account in your plans and then come up with a way to turn it to your advantage.

I glanced upstairs. No sign of Genevieve yet. She might be off getting things ready for the Mensarius, or maybe it was an early dinner. I should be gone before she got back, but if I wasn't, I'd . . . use my yoga skills to move as quietly as I could.

And go where?

To the black market, of course. If I got there ahead of her,

I could make a deal with whoever she was going to sell the memories to. Then it wouldn't matter if she sold them, and I had to have something useful to offer them. My mind was brimming with memories. Board gaming and yoga, for one thing. There would be a way to make a trade.

Trading was a key part of board gaming, after all. I had experience with it. Sort of.

Genevieve still hadn't come back by the time I had a big enough space carved for me to escape. I didn't hesitate a moment, just clambered up out of the hole, scurrying on my fingers and toes underneath the trailer and peering out into the open.

It was late afternoon now. The second I came out and started walking around, I'd attract a ton of attention. A kid covered in dirt and his own filth, with sliced-up wrists and tearstained cheeks? I'd be in protective custody in a heartbeat, and that was bad. Genevieve could come in and pluck me up as easily as a penny off the sidewalk.

So I'd have to make sure not to stay there.

I crept over to each side of the trailer in turn, peering out through the latticework to see which way would be my best exit. On one side, there was a leather goods booth right next to me. Better yet, it was the side that didn't have the line of people waiting for a chance to meet Genevieve. I didn't really love the idea of walking around in leather for the rest of the day, but it was better than any other option I had.

It took a little while for me to carve my way through the lattice, then a bit more for a good time to exit, when no one was coming and no one was looking. Genevieve would be able to see how I got out, but she didn't seem like someone who would worry too much about a twelve-year-old trying to mess up her plans.

Five minutes later, I had exchanged my shirt for a stolen leather jacket and hat. Thieving turned out to be much easier when you could just jump into the merchant's mind and take out any memory that they'd had of that jacket to begin with. Yes, I felt guilty about it, but this was for the greater good. It had to be done, and I'd return it when it was all over.

Whatever I had to tell myself to get through this.

I headed to the bathrooms next, to wash my face and hands and get as presentable as possible. That done, it was time for the next stage of my plan. All I knew was that the Mensarius was coming somewhere here this evening. Going around asking strangers if they'd seen it would be difficult: I'd draw attention to myself, and I didn't know what questions to ask in the first place.

But I didn't have to actually ask any questions at all.

For the next half hour, I jumped in and out of so many memory libraries, I lost count. They came in all shapes and sizes: school rooms, swimming pools, equestrian centers, sports arenas, basements, cubicles, libraries, living rooms, TV control rooms, bowling alleys, mini-golf courses, churches, castles, and more. Each time, I just took a moment to flip through their recent memories, looking to see if they'd seen anything unusual in the last day or so. The search was simple, since all I had to do was focus on the question, then open a drawer or turn a control dial or look in a storage tub to see what came up.

In between, I kept an eye out for Genevieve, of course. Part of me still thought the easiest thing to do would be to confront her head-on, but the board gamer in me told me that was a bad idea. I'd tried it before, and I didn't have a clear path to victory that way. Even though I didn't know for sure if this different plan would work, it was better than a guaranteed failure. I considered finding her, then following her until I knew where she was keeping the rest of the memories, but an ambush just wouldn't work. She'd told me she was an expert in, like, five martial arts.

I could do yoga.

So I stuck to the plan, and I didn't end up seeing Genevieve anyway. I didn't see anything suspicious in those memories, either. Nothing worthwhile, at least. There were images of shoplifters, arguments, traffic violations, and more. Plenty of strangers, but no one who stood out.

And with each memory library I visited, the Whispers started to show up earlier and earlier.

I wasn't sure if it was just because I was going to so many minds with few breaks. What were the Whispers anyway? The defense of the mind against things that shouldn't be there? But if that were the case, shouldn't they not be connected? Each new mind should reset the timer. Then again, Louis had never done what I was doing now. He'd go into minds at a much more leisurely pace.

This was more of an all-out sprint.

And maybe when I went that quickly from mind to mind, I became a bigger and bigger threat. Something each new mind could tell was foreign more quickly, so the defenses shot up right away.

"You're going to lose."

"You don't know what you're doing."

"Your sister will kill herself."

"Your parents are already dead."

The Whispers didn't just come more quickly, they grew more disturbing, too. They moved on from simply taunting me about my self-doubts and fears and evolved into outright threats and terrible images.

"Blood, Benjamin. Blood everywhere."

"You'll find her. Dead. Cold. Stiff."

"Sightless eyes."

"Mouth in a frozen scream."

Trying to stay focused was only getting harder. They

weren't just trying to terrify me, of course. They were trying to get me to really *listen*. To do what they were telling me to do.

"Give up, Benjamin."

"Come over here. Come stand here and rest."

"Look at this bookshelf."

"You're such an expert. Why not fight us? Why not try to win?"

I did my best to just stay focused. In a way, it helped that I was only in each memory library so briefly. But I still caught myself walking over to shelves or corners or aisles that I hadn't intended to, following the Whispers without even thinking about it. Each time, I caught myself. Each time, I checked for what I'd come for and then I fled.

But I could tell I wouldn't be able to do this forever. I needed an answer. A clue. Anything that might tell me where that Mensarius thing was.

People near the center of the fair had nothing for me, so I began to roam the edges. I started over near the livestock, then circled around the trailers and back behind the racetrack. When I was on the far side, I came across one of the caretakers at the fairgrounds, tall and thin enough that you thought he might blow over in a stiff wind. His memory library was a replica of the exhibit hall, with its rows of display cases and grange exhibits. The floor squeaked just as it always did, and it was hot and stuffy even without any people.

The Whispers only made it worse.

As soon as I was in the hall, they began, insistent and unavoidable. "You could beat us if you tried. You're powerful."

The Whispers didn't just use threats, I was discovering. They liked to mix things up. Some people listened to compliments much more easily, and that's all they really wanted. Once you started paying attention to them—once their opinions mattered to you—then they had you. I hurried to a display case. Unlike the ones in real life, these had frosted glass, so you couldn't see what was inside.

"Come over here and test us."

For the hundredth time, I focused on anything strange or unusual the man might have seen, and I opened the case. Inside was a homemade handbag. I frowned, hesitating. A handbag?

"How can you hope to defeat Genevieve if you can't even face us?"

When I took it out and studied it closer, I saw words had been embroidered around the hemlines. This guy won the award for "Strangest Way to Store Your Memories." It made it harder to scan over them for anything that stood out, but I did my best.

"Death."

There was a bunch about people he'd seen in the fair, including a tattooed woman who might have been Genevieve, but he'd seen her right in the middle of the fair, so it wasn't anything that might help me know where the Memoria Mensarius was. The man was certainly paranoid. He found lots to be suspicious about, from a kid who had been in the grandstands by himself, reading a book, to a bunch of Winnebagos that were parked illegally on a street behind the racetrack, the hulking mobile homes crowding out any space for other cars to get by.

"Your parents are already dead. There's nothing you can do."

I was about to put the bag back and move on to the next memory when I glimpsed a piece of writing I'd missed. It was over by the Winnebago section, and the hem had folded in on itself more than elsewhere. I stretched the fabric to get a better look. As soon as I saw "glowing glass bottles," I knew I had something.

The Whispers knew it, too, somehow, and they increased their efforts to trap me. "Put the memory back, Benjamin. Get a new one. A more focused one."

I froze. That was exactly what I'd been planning on doing. I needed a better idea about those Winnebagos. Any extra bit of information could help me. This was a new trick by the Whispers; if I did what they told me to, even though I was already going to, would that make me weaker to them? More susceptible?

Like it or not, I needed those memories. I rushed over to the far end of the hall, away from where the Whispers had been coming from. As soon as I got there, I focused on the Winnebagos—everything the man might know about these particular ones—and opened a display case, hoping this would be enough for me to avoid an ambush.

Inside the case was a model of a Winnebago, carved out of wood. I thrust the bag into the case, grabbed the model, and shut the door.

Too slow.

As the door shut, a shadowy hand whipped out to grab my wrist. "We have you now, Benjamin." The Whispers were sharp and exultant. "Give up."

I fled the man's memory library as fast as I could, though the Whispers seemed to laugh at me as I did, and the feeling of that hand on my wrist was still with me when I was back in the fresh evening air. That had been too much. The first time the Whispers had attacked me, back when I was new to the whole business of Memory Thieving, it had been more by surprise than anything else. They'd been able to get to me because I wasn't prepared.

The sort of sustained mind hopping I'd been doing for the past few hours was a different story. They'd worn down my defenses. Gotten inside my head. The experience I'd gotten from Louis convinced me that the next time I went into another person's mind, the Whispers would be worse than ever. They would be out for blood, and they were guaranteed to get it at this point. I'd given them way too much power, and I'd need to take a break for at least a day or two before I even thought about doing that again.

Hopefully, I wouldn't have to.

The man's memories of the Winnebago caravan were now *my* memories. I knew where they were parked. I knew that the cupboard of the second one on the left was chock full of memory bottles, and that had been the only one the man had seen the inside of.

I glanced at my watch. Seven o'clock. That hunt had taken me longer than I would have liked, but I still had an hour before Genevieve was planning to go to the Mensarius.

It was time to try and make a deal with someone else for a change.

CHAPTER

16

MEMORIA MENSARIUS

When I walked up to the caravan, I tried my best to seem confident. These people would probably try to take advantage of me. I didn't want them to think I would be easy pickings. If I could have, I would have just jumped into their memory libraries as soon as I could make eye contact with them, but with the Whispers as strong as they were by now, that was out of the question.

The Memoria Mensarius wasn't directly behind the fair. It was located a couple of streets over, and it took me some time to get to it. Maine roads didn't exactly always lead where you thought they would. But I still got there with a good half hour to spare.

There were RVs parked on either side of the street. Big, hulking machines in various states of repair. Some were sleek and modern, others seemed to be held together by nothing more than duct tape. There were black ones, silver ones, rusted ones, beige ones, green ones, and brown ones. Fifteen or twenty in all. Some of them were running, puffing out clouds of exhaust into the fresh air.

The people who lived on this street must have loved that. Then I noticed some of those people, standing on their front lawns, idly clutching at rakes or just staring into the night air. All of them had eyes completely black from memory theft. These people hadn't just been stolen from. They'd been cleaned out completely.

The owners of the RVs, on the other hand, were easy to identify. They'd built a bonfire in the middle of the street and were lazing around in camp chairs, roasting hot dogs and marshmallows, smoking and drinking and laughing it up. They were a group as mixed as their vehicles. Some wore overalls and T-shirts, others were in nicer dresses. I saw one man in a tie. They were old, young, fat, thin, black, white: about forty of them in all.

As I approached, someone must have finished a joke. The group erupted in laughter, but it was a harsher laughter than you'd hear around a normal campfire. It had an edge to it, as if the joke had come at someone's expense.

It wasn't a good first impression.

A short, fat man dressed in a grease-stained Red Sox shirt noticed me when I was about fifteen feet away. He jerked his head at me while looking at the others. "Here comes another one," he said. "I've got it. Again." His voice had a thick Downeast Maine drawl.

He cleared his throat and hauled himself to his feet, trotting a few steps in my direction before holding his hand up and waving me forward. "Come on," he said. "Might as well not stand there forever, mouth open, catching flies. Let me see your eyes, son."

I didn't vary my pace. Just kept walking forward, staring straight ahead. I had to show them I meant business. I couldn't be taken advantage of. The old Benji—the Benji from just a few days ago—would never have done this. He'd have found someone else to go talk to these people. Probably Kelly. The new Benji didn't have time to be scared of strangers.

The man fixed me with a hard stare once I was close enough, his body backlit by the fire, making it look like he was burning around the edges. A sharp pain lanced through my head, and I knew he'd tried to jump into my mind. He grunted and stumbled back a step before catching himself.

Some of the others laughed again, and the man glared at them before turning back to me.

"Sorry about that. Didn't realize you was one of us. Bit young, aren't you?"

"Old enough," I said, holding his stare and hoping my voice sounded more confident than I thought it did.

The people were quiet around the fire, staring at me. The man paused for a few beats, then nodded. "That you are, I suppose. What brings you to the Mensarius?"

"I'm here for a trade," I said.

The man gave me a long pause, then turned around to look at the other people around the fire. They stared back at him, stone-faced. He responded, "These aren't trading times, and this ain't a trading place. We're here for pickup and payment. You ought to know that, if you knew anything about us in the first place. To be honest, I'm surprised to see another Memory Thief up here at all. We were only expecting the one of you."

I had a feeling he was being vague on purpose, not mentioning Genevieve's name for some reason. "That's changed," I said.

The man grunted. "Clearly."

Another pause. The fire crackled in the background. One of the people took a hot dog out of the flames. It was blackened and blistered.

I didn't have time for this. Yes, I'd probably do something foolish or say something I wasn't supposed to, but there was no way I was going to be able to bluff my way through this. Now it was my turn to clear my throat. "Genevieve is coming here in a half hour. She's going to sell you some memories. I want them."

"For the love, Angus," a woman said. "Take the business inside. Don't stand here jawing away all night."

Angus nodded, then leaned his head to the left. "Why don't you step inside my office, boy, and we can discuss things a little more in private?"

Following a stranger into his RV was pretty much at the top of the list of Things You Are Never Supposed to Do. But so was getting your twin's memories stolen. I was past the point of being able to worry about stranger danger.

Angus led me to a particularly old and rusty RV. The door opened with a loud screech, falling partway off its hinges before he slammed it back into place. "Sorry about that. Have to get an oil can in here some time. Been busy." He gestured for me to go inside.

The RV smelled of stale burritos and had at least fifty Mountain Dew cans littering the floor. I had to kick some aside just to walk, and all the chairs but one were covered in mounds of newspapers from all over the world. I spotted some Asian ones I couldn't identify, as well as some in

Hebrew, Arabic, and who knew what else.

Angus ambled around me and picked up a pile off a chair, throwing it on the floor. "Have a seat."

"I don't have time," I said.

He shrugged and sat down, plopping his feet up on a nearby mound of paper. "Fair enough. You in such a big hurry, then let's hurry."

I nodded. "Genevieve. She stole the memories of my family, and I want to get them back."

Angus yawned, not even bothering to cover his mouth. "'Scuse me. All their memories, or just some?"

"Some at first, but then all of them earlier today."

He sucked at the side of his lips, thinking. "How many family members?"

"My parents and my twin sister."

Another pause. A couple of flies zoomed by, buzzing loudly in the quiet of the RV. "That's a mite bit expensive, what you're talking about trading," Angus said at last. "Two grown adults, got to figure they're in their thirties, give or take, plus ten years or so of a child. What do you have to offer in return?"

I swallowed. Somehow part of me had assumed once I brought to light what Genevieve was up to, other people would be outraged by this. But Angus was taking it so matter-of-factly. "I . . . I could trade some of my own memories."

He shook his head. "Even if I drained you to the last drop, boy, there's no way I'm getting a fair shake out of that trade. Unless, of course, you were willing to let the ability go."

"The ability?"

"To steal memories. That would be worth a whole town's worth of memories, if you did that."

That rocked me back. Give up the ability? I'd do it in a heartbeat if it would guarantee that my parents and Kelly were back to normal. But it brought the same troubles with it that had made me refuse Genevieve when she made the same offer. "How would I know you wouldn't take more memories than what I wanted to give?"

"You wouldn't."

"And how could I be sure my family would get their memories back?"

"You couldn't."

It felt wrong. Just because the man had a Maine accent didn't make him any more trustworthy. I shook my head. "Couldn't you just use the ability to do this to more people?"

"Ayuh." Mainer for "yes." He continued, a smile on his scruffy face. "Would it help if I crossed my heart?"

"What other options do I have?"

Angus thought for a few moments. "Well, you could pay us for them outright. We'd probably waive the delivery fee, as you're already here and all. And I might be able to talk them down from the full handling fee. Betty would still have to do the once-over on them to make sure all was in place, and Betty don't work cheap, you understand. But even with them discounts, it's still going to be ten, twenty thousand. Each for the parents. Less for the littler one. Say, thirty-five total?"

It was all I could do to stay standing. Memories were that expensive? "I don't have nearly that much."

"You could steal it, of course." Angus was thinking out loud, staring at the ceiling while he spoke. "Not too hard, for a full-fledged Memory Thief. Alls you do is jump in, grab the account numbers and PINs, and jump out. You could have that much and more in about . . . an hour out here. Maybe less, maybe more. Depending on the people you're jumping in and out of. I'm told some of them folks have actual money round here."

"I can't do that. It isn't right."

He gave me a wide grin, revealing a few missing teeth. "That ain't stopped none of your kind before. You get caught, you just steal the memories of the catching, too."

"Why doesn't Genevieve just do that for her money, then?"

Angus raised his eyebrows. "Memory Thieves don't come to the Memoria Mensarius for money. They come for the memories." He hauled himself out of his chair and walked over to the kitchen area, opening a cabinet. It was filled to the brim with glowing bottles, mainly shades of purple and red. "These here? Straight from the Middle Ages. My specialty. You want jousts or chivalry, you come to the right mobile home. This shelf right here is worth over fifty million to the right buyers."

"Then why aren't you dressed better?" I asked. "Why don't you live someplace nicer?"

His face darkened quickly. "Might be I like the way I dress and the way I live. Might be some of us don't care too much for some things. Now, are you going to pay me or just stand there insulting my way of life?"

"I can't," I said. "I won't steal, and I need my memories."

Angus nodded once, then shut the cabinet door. "In that case, I advise you run along before she gets here. Genevieve ain't one for jawing much, and she don't take a shine to people getting in her way."

My stomach sank, and I scrambled to think of another alternative. "What if—what if I sell Genevieve's memories to you instead?"

Silence fell over the RV once again. Angus stared at me, his brow furrowed in disbelief. "You," he said at last. "You think you're going to go up against that woman and come out on top?"

"Would you do it?" I asked.

"What memories are we talking about? Specifically."

"Not the ability to steal memories. And nothing she learned

211

on her own through normal living. All the rest of the stuff. The martial arts she says she can do. Everything she's stolen that can't be returned back to its rightful owner."

Angus grunted. "You'd do that?"

I glared at him. "In a heartbeat."

He rubbed at his chin again, leaning back against the cabinets. "And how do you think you might go about pulling something like that off?"

"Well," I said after a moment. "Do you have any spare skills I could use?"

"Nothing that might be that helpful," Angus said. "I ain't going to give away for free what she's just going to steal back and sell to me in ten minutes."

"What?"

"Son, I don't know where you got the ability to do what you can do now, but I guarantee you don't have half a clue when it comes to using it, and you're about to go up against a woman that not one of those people you sneered at outside would even think about going up against. Genevieve gives wolves and sharks the shakes. If I give you some ninja-level ability, three things are going to happen. One, she's going to beat you senseless anyway. Two, she's going to steal that memory back and make me pay extra for it. And three, she's going to know I helped you. None of those seem like things I'm too eager to have happen, so no. I will not let you have any 'spare skills.'"

When he put it that way, it sounded even bleaker. I tried not to pay attention to it. I had no other choice. "Well," I said, "if you're too scared to—"

He burst out laughing. "You got grit, I'll give you that much. I ain't scared. I'm *smart*. But I'll tell you what. You want, I can let you rummage through the old lost and found. Maybe something there will tickle your fancy."

"The lost and found?"

"Not everything we pick up is something we care that much about. All those odds and ends have to end up somewhere. You see something there you like, it's yours."

All that board-gaming experience ought to come in handy somehow. Maybe it could give me some ways to cobble something together to help me come out on top. "Show me," I said.

He led me outside to a different RV. After his personal vehicle, I hadn't thought it would be possible to get any worse. Angus proved me wrong. His RV had been held together with duct tape. This one had taken away even that. The front fender was falling off, one of the tires looked on its last gasp, and the door was made out of cardboard. When the two of us stepped inside, the whole thing squeaked and squealed and tilted, making me wonder if it might tip over right then. I lunged out to grab hold of the door frame, catching myself at the last second when I noticed it had been torn away, leaving jagged edges in its wake. Thankfully, my yoga-enhanced reflexes managed to keep me from falling over, and the RV itself stayed upright as well.

Inside, a woman sat on a couch that had been ripped to shreds at some point in the distant past, after which it had begun to rot. Black, molding stuffing oozed out of it in several spots, and one of the arms had been ripped off. The woman didn't seem to mind. She sat there, watching a television that had been turned to static. Its hissing and buzzing filled the small space with noise.

Her eyes were completely black, and one of her hands picked at the stuffing absently, while her lips muttered something continually under her breath.

Other than the couch and the television, the room was empty. No cupboards. No kitchen. Just bare walls with peeling wallpaper, and holes in the floor where built-in furniture might have lived at some point in the past.

"Where is it?" I asked Angus.

The woman shrieked in response. I jerked back from her, but her eyes stayed glued to the screen.

"You're looking at it," Angus said, gesturing to the woman with his thumb. "Lost and found. Available twenty-four seven."

I recoiled from the thought. "You just—use her as a storage bank?"

Angus shrugged. "She wasn't doing anything different. Nothing we were interrupting, leastwise. Vegetable in a loony bin's just as happy as a vegetable in a trailer. Memories cost money to store, boy. Them bottles ain't exactly free. She can store as much as we want, and we don't need to worry about her taking them and selling 'em on." He glanced at a nonexistent watch on his wrist. "Time's ticking. You want to riffle through what we got or not?"

It wasn't even a debate, and not just because I knew that if I tried to go into her mind, the Whispers would be waiting for me. There were right things in the world and wrong things, and what they'd done to this woman was nothing but wrong. It was like I was staring at all my problems with Memory Thieves, all compacted into one individual. If this was what the Memoria Mensarius was all about, I wanted nothing to do with it, other than to do everything I could to shut it down.

Genevieve wasn't only a small slice of the problem, it seemed. But she was the only slice I could handle right now, and I wasn't even sure I'd be able to handle that.

"No," I said at last. "No deal."

Angus grunted. "Well. I can't say it's been nice knowing you, as I haven't, but I'll wish you the best of luck anyway. You come across any memories you want to unload, you know where you can find us. Just be aware that if you try to cross us or stop us ever, we have ways of dealing with that." He gestured at the woman, who was still muttering, still picking at that stuffing.

Had they *punished* her for something?

It was all I could do not to lose my lunch right there. Without another word, I stumbled out the door and back into the evening air.

C H A P T E R

17

LAST CHANCE

Nothing. That's what I was left with. I'd escaped from Genevieve's pit, I'd scrambled to find a way to defeat her, and now I was standing in the middle of the road, waiting for her to show up, and I didn't have one bit of a clue about what to do.

The members of the Mensarius had made fun of me as I hurried off, calling me names ranging from "young'un" to things I didn't want to ever repeat, let alone remember. I made sure to get as much space away from them as I could, worried that one or more of them might be willing to team up with Genevieve for a cut of the profits. Going up against a master Memory Thief was one thing. I didn't need to complicate matters by getting stabbed in the back.

I stopped myself. "Master Memory Thief." Wasn't that what I was as well? I had all of Louis's abilities, after all. But it seemed like he hadn't been able to transfer all the experience he'd had. Just the knowledge. It was like I had a great grasp of all the textbook answers but didn't have enough of a start on the application of them.

You'd think that wouldn't make much of a difference, but it did. If I'd had real experience, there was no way I would have done what I did to my parents. And there was no way I'd be as nervous as I was right then.

I was going to lose. I didn't just have a bad plan, I had *no* plan. Almost nothing to work with, either. Just Louis's memories, and the ability to win board games and do yoga stretches. It was like I had a hard test coming up, and I hadn't even cracked the book to skim through the material. Worse: at least on a test, I could just guess at an answer.

How could I guess now? Genevieve would show up, and—

She stepped out of the darkness, striding toward me, her face still covered in shadows. I swallowed, wishing I felt even a little more confident. Wishing I didn't feel like my doom was approaching.

"Benjamin!" she exclaimed. "Fancy meeting you here!"

I licked my lips and clenched my jaw, waiting for her to come closer before I said anything. "I want my family's memories back. I want the whole town's memories. You leave Livingston and never come back."

She smiled at me. Those tattoos on her arms seemed to glow in the faint firelight, twisted images of beheadings and torture and witches burned at the stake. "Finally decided to sell, have we? How do you know the offer's still on the table?"

"Because I'm the only one who can give them to you."

Genevieve reached into her back pocket and pulled out a bottle that glowed with a deep-blue intensity I'd never seen before. It was the sort of blue you just wanted to sit and stare at forever. To think about it. A blue that promised secrets, if you could only decode them. Could it really be even more intense outside of the bottle, like she said? It was hard to believe. "I brought this down to the pit to use on you. That concentrated amnesia I was telling you about? Imagine my disappointment to see you'd scurried off without saying good-bye."

"You don't need to wipe my memories," I said. "I'll give you what you want, if you give me what I want." What was I saying? This woman couldn't be trusted. The moment I let her into my mind, she'd go to town on the place. I'd be more picked over than a Walmart after Black Friday.

She glanced at the bottle, then back to me, considering. "It *would* save me some work," she said at last. "You'd really go through with it?"

My mind was screaming at me to do something else. Run for it. Tackle her. Scream for help. Anything. But somewhere deep inside me, Louis's memories seemed to contradict those urges. I stuck my hand out for Genevieve to take, and when I did, it felt right somehow.

It felt good.

Maybe I was going crazy, or Genevieve might have brainwashed me somehow. Was that possible? But all I had were those instincts, so I kept my hand outstretched, waiting.

Genevieve studied it as if she thought it might hide a trap, but in the end, she accepted the handshake. I opened my mind to her—

And we were inside my memory library.

Where the Whispers had been waiting.

The moment we arrived, their voices practically screamed into the silence, harsh raspy tones cutting through the air.

"We knew you'd be back."

"Hello, Benjamin. Come over to the bookshelf."

And, more surprisingly, "Genevieve. It's been a long time."

She stumbled back, her eyes wide with surprise. "What have you been doing?" she asked me.

In response, I lunged forward and shoved her as hard as I could toward the sound of the Whispers. She shrieked, but I jumped out of my mind as soon as I'd done it, her voice getting cut off as I went back to the real world.

I gasped when I was back outside, my hand clenched tight in Genevieve's fist. Her eyes were closed, a look of determination and struggle painted across her face. It was all I could do not to panic. She was inside me right now. In my head, with full access to my memories. Sure, the Whispers might hold her off for a moment or two, but I had to assume she'd be better at fighting them than I was.

Whatever I was going to do, I only had moments to do it. My eyes darted around for inspiration, immediately settling upon the glowing blue bottle in Genevieve's other hand.

I reached out and plucked it from her hand just as she took a breath and opened her eyes, letting go of my hand in the process. And yes, maybe those yoga skills came in handy in that quick movement. If I could just get this done before she stole my—

I blinked, staring around me in confusion.

"What are you doing, young man?" the woman in front of me asked.

Where was I, and why was I alone with a strange woman at night? "I . . ." My mind raced, trying to come up with an answer, but it only hit a blank wall. It felt like I'd been doing something important. Something vital, just moments before. But like a question you wanted to ask for hours but then forgot at the last moment, it was gone completely. "I'm not sure," I said at last. "Who are you?"

The woman smiled at me. "Just a concerned neighbor. I think you might have hit your head. Why don't we go over to that fire and see if someone has a phone so we can call a doctor?"

I glanced behind me. In the distance, a group of RVs were parked on either side of the street, a bonfire blazing between them, right in the middle of the road. Why did the sight of that make me uneasy? I put my hand up to my head, only then noticing that it held a bottle of some sort. A bottle that glowed blue in the darkness. Where had that come from, and what was it? Some kind of party favor?

"Come on," the woman said, her smile growing wider. (Too wide?) "Why don't you give that to me, and we can go get you some help. Those people are my friends. They'll be able to fix you up."

She put a hand on my shoulder, and I flinched without knowing why. It must have been because I was so confused. It didn't feel like I'd hit my head or anything. Wasn't that what happened with amnesia? But why did my eyes fall down to stare at the glowing blue bottle when I thought about amnesia?

"I think I need to go to a hospital," I said.

The woman tsked. "That won't be necessary. I'm sure we can help you. If you'd just sit down, you'll feel better. It's probably low blood sugar. Give me the bottle."

And why shouldn't I give it to her? I didn't know what it was anyway. I shrugged and held the bottle out to her, and her eyes flashed with triumph. She went to take it from my hands, but my grip wouldn't loosen. It was like my hand didn't want to do what my brain was telling it to.

"Let it go, Benji," she said, her voice tense with displeasure.

Benji? Was that who I was? "No," I said, and pulled back on the bottle.

The woman hissed in frustration and yanked harder. I stepped into the pull, throwing her off balance in surprise. She brought her left hand up in a fist and punched me in the nose. It was so sudden and unexpected. Pain blossomed across my face, and I let go of the bottle to cradle my head.

She let out a long sigh. "At last." I looked up to see her with her eyes closed, bottle in hand, a satisfied smile on her face. "I thought I'd never be able to—"

I hurtled forward into her, hitting her squarely in the chest. The air blew out from her lungs in an explosion, and the two of us fell to the pavement. We rolled around on the ground for a moment. Her knees jabbed up into my stomach, and her arm snaked itself around my neck faster than I thought possible. The woman was far stronger than I was, but I *stretched* in a certain way, and the pressure on my windpipe loosened just enough for me to twist free for a moment.

Screaming for help didn't occur to me. All I could think

of was getting that bottle back and . . . breaking it. Smashing it open, as if it would free me from something I couldn't remember. Something so important that I was willing to do anything to get it. My life was in danger, even though I couldn't understand why.

I gripped the woman's arm in my hands and clamped down on it as hard as I could with my teeth, biting deep into the tattoo-covered flesh.

Now she was the one to cry out, and her arm spasmed and dropped the bottle. It fell to the ground with a dull *clink*, and I turned around, trying as hard as I could to reach it before she got me.

My fingertips brushed at the edges, knocking the bottle just out of reach. The woman got to her feet and kicked me in the side, however, the pain intense. I fought against the urge to curl into a ball. If I didn't get that bottle—

I stretched one more time and grabbed hold of it just as three more kicks came raining into my stomach, kidney, and shoulder. Whoever the woman was, she knew how to inflict pain. I rolled away, my body somehow having enough control over itself to still keep its bearings.

Without thinking, I raised the bottle up and brought it smashing down onto the asphalt as hard as I could.

Glass shattered, and the blue glow inside the bottle hung in the air for a moment, tendrils of it testing the wind, as if it were hesitating. Thinking.

The woman gasped and backpedaled away from it as if it were a poisonous snake.

I did the same thing, skittering on my hands and feet like a crab. Somehow my hands had managed to get through the glass breaking without getting sliced. At least, I didn't think they had. It was hard to focus.

All my attention was on that blue mist. Watching it weave back and forth in the air. Light. Effortless. In fact, why was I wanting to be anywhere else? I could stay here forever, just staring at the wonderful blue. So dark. So deep.

On the other side of the mist, some part of me registered the fact that the woman had slowed down as well, staring at the same mist. It had gotten even more intense now that it was out of that bottle. The light was bright enough to bathe the area in its glow. The woman's jaw hung slack, and her eyes followed that mist the same way mine did.

I wasn't sure how long we stood there frozen, the mist hanging in the air between us. It might have been seconds, it might have been hours.

But then it began to move.

I had to bite back a groan of disappointment as it sunk to the ground and then slithered its way toward the woman. Why had it chosen her? Why not me? Had I done something wrong? Angered it? Disappointed it?

The blue mist was rising from the ground. It traced a line up the woman's leg and looped around her waist. She laughed as it came closer to her head, every line of her face outlined with that blue glow.

And then it twisted, tightening. Her face changed from smiles to terror in an instant. "What did you—" was all she got out before the blue shot plunged into her face.

There were no screams. No pyrotechnics. Just a woman standing there as a glowing blue stream flowed into her eyes, nose, and mouth.

The pyrotechnics came after that.

The woman froze, staring into nothing. Two seconds later, she erupted in a blinding white light, scattered with hints of every color of the rainbow. There was no sound. Just a constant stream of light that filled the whole area. I could see images in it. Brief glimpses from the woman's past, perhaps. Her first steps. Her father. Riding a bike. Kissing a boy at school. All in rapid succession.

And then all of it headed straight at me. It was like the blue light had caused it to burst out of her, and it needed someplace to go. I was the closest thing. I cringed in fear as it rushed at me, the light getting stronger and stronger until it was like trying to look at the sun in the middle of the day. My eyes hurt, and I clenched them closed.

CHAPTER

18

RESET

It was hard to make sense of all of them. Everything Genevieve had known—all her memories, all her skills—flooded into my mind like a fire hose shooting water into a goldfish bowl.

It was like it had been with Louis but way more expansive. I knew everything about Genevieve. I *remembered* it all. And just like my experience with Mom and Dad's anger at each other, the reality of Genevieve's life was much more different than I'd pictured it.

Growing up in Pennsylvania. Elementary school. Learning to play the clarinet. Meeting Louis at the Grange Fair and running away from home to train with him. It turned out Louis had been selective about the memories he gave me. I'd thought they'd been everything he had about Memory Thieving, but he'd definitely left out the training of Genevieve. He'd given me nothing about the times he'd beat her. The short temper he'd had. The way he'd taught her how to bilk people out of their memories.

He'd done the same thing she'd been doing. Stolen memories from people, agreeing to pay and then going back on his promises. He'd been a pretty nasty piece of work.

And then Genevieve (or was it me? Whose memories were these?) had tricked him into giving her some of his memories—basically doing to him what I'd done to my parents. She'd been trying to cure him. To make him a better person. And it had worked, but it had also corrupted me—her. She'd stolen key parts of Louis's memories and most of his money, and headed out on her own, taking over his connections and his routes. Making money of her own.

She'd had more than just her own memories in her head. She knew far more than any twenty-year-old could have. A wealth of talents, for one thing. Perfect marksmanship. How to speak thirty different languages. Twelve different martial arts. Complex theoretical physics. She'd made a habit of collecting the most interesting tidbits of memories from the people she'd stolen from, keeping them for herself.

And now those memories were mine. *I* knew how to speak Swahili and Tagalog. *I* was an expert stunt driver. *I* knew how to break into just about any safe in the world. All those memories also made it easier for me to keep being me. Being Benji. Genevieve had so many memories that outweighed her own. I hadn't just taken on twenty years of memories. It was more like one hundred, but it had come with the skill and experience needed to handle all those memories. To keep them separate from my own. Louis had just shoved in what he could in the few moments he had. Genevieve had given it all to me. She'd had no choice.

I discovered that Genevieve had been hiding some elements of Memory Thieving from me. Limitations she didn't want to let on that she had. The fact that she had to rest for weeks at a time after she stole too many at once. The crippling migraines that could fall on her at any time. There were consequences of being a Memory Thief, and the more often you used the power, the more you came to depend on it. It was like a drug. Genevieve couldn't stop herself. It *twisted* you after you did it too long. She hadn't come to the fair because there were such valuable memories to steal here. She'd come because if she drained herself out on all these lesser memories, she'd be less desperate for a fix when she lived in the city. Like an alcoholic avoiding bars when he knew he'd want a drink.

Genevieve stealing Louis's memories had saved him from the person he had become. Perhaps my taking Genevieve's memories would do the same thing for her, in the long run. I'd just have to be sure I didn't let them corrupt me in the same way.

Maybe being a great Memory Thief wasn't all I'd thought it would be after all.

As all those memories came to me, they brought Genevieve's expertise of Memory Thieving, in addition to the stolen pieces she'd taken from Louis. I knew how to put memories into bottles. How to mix them like cocktails to get a desired result. I knew that they really *did* degrade over time—she hadn't been lying about that. Inside a person's mind was one thing, but out in a bottle was something much different.

Ironically, Louis had taught me how to steal memories, but it was Genevieve who taught me how to give them back quickly and effectively.

When I had all the memories more or less under control, I opened my eyes. The darkness of early night around us seemed pitch-black in comparison to the light Genevieve's memories had given off. She was sprawled on the ground, staring up at the sky, her arms and legs spasming in a way that reminded me of newborns, as if she had no control over her limbs.

She started crying. Not a controlled sob or hysterical scream. Just random bursts of cries—again, just like a baby.

I walked over to her. "Genevieve?"

She didn't even glance in my direction. Her limbs kept flailing, and the cries kept coming. This was what she'd planned to do to me? This was terrible. Completely steal every ounce of a person's life and leave them helpless? If I did nothing, she'd get locked up in a mental facility. It would take years for her to recover even a shred of a normal life.

And I couldn't do that—not even to someone like Genevieve.

We'd been attracting some attention from the Mensarius behind us. With the pyrotechnics and screams, we were probably attracting attention from people at the fair, too. A small group had gathered about twenty feet away, Angus at the head of it.

"Bring me a bottle," I shouted out. My voice sounded different. More mature. More commanding.

Angus stepped forward, an empty bottle held in his outstretched hand. I knew him now. Genevieve knew him. He was as honest as anyone in the Mensarius, which didn't mean much. But he was also a coward at heart, and the sort of man who would gladly stab a friend in the back if the price was right.

I snatched the bottle from him. "Go back to your bonfire,"

I said to the group. "There'll be nothing for you from this tonight."

And for some reason, all of them did what I said. No questions asked. Angus hesitated for a moment, staring at me, and I thought he might actually say something, but in the end he nodded, turned, and left. What did my face look like now? What sort of expression made other people act that way?

I inspected the empty bottle, moving it around in my hands. Then I concentrated on Genevieve's core memories. Learning to walk. Talk. First kiss. School lessons. There was a feel each person's memories had to them. Like a fingerprint, but more abstract. If you were familiar enough with the process, you could tell where everything had come from, even once those memories degraded for a few years. (Memories stolen decades ago were almost impossible to trace.) Memories that had been taken mere minutes before?

Piece of cake.

I avoided the dangerous memories. Anything that touched on Memory Thieving, for one thing. It would be better for Genevieve and the world in general if she never came across that ability again. I also didn't give back her stolen memories. So she wasn't going to be an Olympic-level champion in multiple sports anymore. Her days of cooking at an elite level were over, too.

Anything she'd experienced on her own, I gave back (with

the exception of what she'd learned from Louis). I put it all into that bottle, and as I did, the bottle filled with a silvery mist as the memories transferred from my mind to my fingers to the bottle, a complicated process that took years to master.

Unless you took shortcuts.

Once I finished, I reviewed all the memories in my head to see if I'd missed anything. I checked the bottle one more time, too, making sure the memories there were safe. It was a different experience, working with the bottles. No library involved, for one thing, and thank goodness. The Whispers would have had a field day with me in this condition. Instead of having to bring someone into my memory library, it was more like going through a mental file cabinet. Genevieve had been an expert at looking at and analyzing the memories in her possession, separating them out. She'd stolen that knowledge from Louis.

I had it now.

The bottle was good to go.

Genevieve was still thrashing and wailing on the ground. I sighed, then walked to stand over her and pour the bottle out. There were enough memories in there that I knew they'd drop straight down. The shimmering mist descended, looping a time or two on its way before plunging into Genevieve's screaming face. As I waited for it to drop, I filled the bottle once again, this time with the harmful memories Genevieve had trapped me with earlier. No need to be burdened with that.

When I was done, the crying had stopped.

"Hello?" I said.

"Who's there?" Genevieve asked.

"Are you okay?"

"Where am I?" She frowned. I'd kept her memories of the past month. She stood up. I saw her arms in the faint light. The same tattoos were there, a hodgepodge of pictures and color, though they seemed less sinister now. Was that because I was no longer afraid of her?

I explained to Genevieve that I'd heard her crying and came to see what was happening. She asked for explanations. I didn't give any. I walked with her to a security booth at the fair. There was no way I'd leave her with the Mensarius. It would have been nice if I could have plucked her memories of the past few minutes out of her head. I didn't want any police asking questions about me, but I didn't dare. Not with the Whispers. But I didn't think it would matter too much. She'd been taking people's memories of her away from them as she went around the fair yesterday. No one would recognize her. No one would tell her what she'd been doing.

I didn't feel guilty about Genevieve. I'd given her a new

chance at life. A shot at doing it right. It was much more than she'd given other people over the years. Much more than she'd planned on giving me.

Social services could look out for her for a while until she was back on her feet. In the meantime, I had other things to do—like going back to her trailer and finding a few more empty bottles as fast as possible. There'd be time for restoring the town's stolen memories later. Family first.

CHAPTER

19

SPILLED MILK

It was almost midnight by the time I got home. In my backpack, I had three bottles, one for each of my family members. I had the keys to Genevieve's trailer in my pocket.

The front door to my house hung ajar, and when I eased it open, the television was blasting from the living room. An infomercial, from the sound of it.

I edged in, not sure of what I'd find. Kelly and my parents had been without any happy memories for almost half the day. It had almost ruined me to feel that deep depression for just a few minutes. What would I have done if it had lasted hours?

The kitchen was in shambles. Someone had left the refrigerator open, and it was humming loudly as it tried in vain to keep the food cool. A gallon of milk had been spilled all over the table, and Cheerios were scattered across the floor.

"Kelly?" I called out. "Mom? Dad?"

I glanced back at the hallway, wondering if they'd gone upstairs. Better to check the living room first. At least I'd be able to turn off that television. And if the house had been broken into . . . I wasn't exactly helpless anymore. Memory Thieving was still out, but I could use some of the martial arts expertise I'd inherited from Genevieve.

I made my way through the kitchen, my feet crunching on the spilled cereal.

Kelly was sitting on the couch, staring at the television. Her eyes were black orbs, and there were streaks on her face where tears had dried unwiped. Her hair was uncombed, and it looked like she hadn't done anything since she got home yesterday other than stare at that television. Well, that and eat some Cheerios and ice cream. A half-eaten bowl of cereal sat beside her on the couch, and an almost full tub of liquid Rocky Road was in her lap.

"Kelly?" I rushed to her side.

She didn't respond.

Not for the first time, I cursed Genevieve and the way she had treated people. How was a person supposed to live with all their happy memories gone? And she'd done that to my family out of simple spite. It was such a horrid thing to do to someone—anyone.

"Don't worry, Kelly," I said. "I'll fix this."

My hands trembled as I opened up my backpack and took out the bottles with my family's memories. I eyed each one until I found Kelly's, then licked my lips, rubbed my palms on my cargo pants, and unstopped the bottle.

It was filled with a raging tornado of contrasting colors. Memories only settled into a single color after they'd had time to sit for several weeks or months. This concoction was too fresh for that. It had all of Kelly's happiness—from the first time she rode a bike to the joy she got from eating her favorite flavor of ice cream. Add all her memories of me from birth to a few days ago, and there was a lot kicking around in that bottle.

Transferring it back to Kelly had some risks. When I'd put the memories back into Genevieve a few hours ago, it had been simple because they'd left her mind so recently. They knew where they belonged, and they went back home. Even the space of a few hours between when you stole the memories and when you put them back could be difficult. You had to do it just right, or a person could become completely insane, convinced that all their memories were lies.

I didn't want that to happen to Kelly.

Thankfully, Genevieve had done this plenty of times. The trick was to start to enter their mind as if you were about to steal their memories, but to pause right on the cusp. Not in their mind, but not out of it. Perched on that knife's edge, the Whispers wouldn't be able to sense me, and I'd be able to direct the memories back where they belonged. It was more by feel than anything else, like doing a jigsaw puzzle in the dark.

If the memories Genevieve had stolen had been minor ones, I wouldn't have risked this. But the alternative—Kelly had no will to live. I had to fix this.

I took a breath, held it, and began pouring out the memories into Kelly a dribble at a time. It was like pouring maple syrup into each square of a waffle, but the maple syrup was in a punch bowl, and you couldn't afford to let even one drop of it spill into the wrong square. And you were blindfolded. At the same time, I also had to be on the lookout for the false memories Genevieve had left there. Kelly didn't want to still think she was Sam's girlfriend, after all.

It seemed to take forever, my mind focused on sifting and placing each memory in the right spot. As I did, I understood things about my sister that I hadn't before. You think you know a person, growing up with them, sharing the same birthday, experiencing the same things, but it's different for everyone. Her memories contrasted with mine, even contradicted them at times. I remembered our Christmas two years ago as an awesome day, when we'd just sat back and played video games until our fingers blistered. Kelly didn't. For her, it was a day she'd spent struggling. She'd overheard Mom and Dad arguing in the bedroom, talking about a divorce. It was the first time that word had come up that she could remember, and it had upset her almost to the point of tears.

She'd pretended not to know anything, even to me. She didn't want my Christmas ruined, and she'd never mentioned it afterward.

That wasn't the only example. There were arguments we'd had, movies we'd watched, friendships she'd experienced. All of them different from her perspective. In that sifting process on the couch, I got to know my twin in a way I never could have before. It made me worry all the more that I'd mess something up.

The world needed more people like Kelly, not fewer.

Once I'd finished, I sat back from her, examining her body language. She was still on the couch, but her eyes were closed. Were her shoulders still slumping as much as they had been? Had I done it right? It was one thing to have Genevieve's memories of how it was done. It was another to use them myself.

"Kelly?" I asked, afraid what the response might be.

Her eyelids fluttered open, and she took a deep breath and looked around the room. But they were still black. No sign of white or color in them. Had I messed up? Did she even know where she was?

"What's my name?" I asked.

She stared forward, ignoring the question.

My stomach dropped a few feet. "What's my name?" I repeated.

Kelly slowly turned to face me, then frowned. Was the question that difficult for her? I couldn't tell with those black eyes just staring at me. I must have done something wrong. It could take them a few moments to clear up, but surely not this long.

"Where are you?" I tried instead. "Do you know where this is?"

She cocked an eyebrow and looked at me like I was crazy. "Is today Stupid Question Day or what, Benji? Sheesh." She blinked a couple of times, and the black color drained away until I was staring into her wonderfully normal eyes again.

I threw my arms around her in a bear hug, ignoring her as she asked, "Do you know what country we're in? Is the sky blue outside? What is peanut butter?"

I broke off the hug, holding her out at arm's length to inspect her. "Are you okay? What do you remember?"

She frowned in thought for a moment. "Did I . . . *kiss* Sam Hyde?"

241

My jaw dropped open. That hadn't been one of the memories I gave her. "Did you?"

Kelly blushed, shaking her head. "Never mind. I remember that woman stealing my memories. Part of me still doesn't want to believe it, but . . . I know what happened. And Mom and Dad were acting like complete space cadets. Can you help them?"

I nodded. "I think so."

Our parents were in their bedroom, lying next to each other, both of them asleep. Their room was dark, the curtains drawn, the television off. They were still in their street clothes—they hadn't even taken off their shoes before lying down. Seeing them next to each other in bed was a rarity. They hadn't shared the same bedroom in two years.

"So they don't remember being mad at each other at all?" Kelly asked.

I shook my head. "They also don't remember being happy. Ever. I can fix it, though."

As I was reaching into my backpack for another bottle of memories, Kelly touched my arm. "Fix all of it?" she asked, her expression intent.

I shrugged. "It's the only way."

"But . . ." Her voice trailed off, and then she continued, speaking quickly. "But they said they wanted to divorce and maybe split us up. Can't you do something about that?"

"I can't say I haven't thought about it," I told her. "But it's not right. If we're going to fix the problems our family has, we're not going to be able to do it through picking and choosing what our parents can remember. We're going to have to talk."

"But can't we—"

I shook my head. "People *earn* memories through living, and they make you what you are. Besides, people always end up repeating the same mistakes. You can pretend all you want that if you could go back in time, you'd do better than you did the first time, but it's not true. We are who we are, and that is what it is." Genevieve's and Louis's memories both told me that, and my gut said they weren't lying.

And although Kelly stared at our parents for a few beats, she eventually nodded. "Okay."

Now that I'd already done this with Kelly, I was more confident with my parents. I had to wake them both up, of course—it couldn't be done without eye contact. But I got them through it in one piece. If I'd thought I was tired after Kelly, I was on a whole new plane of exhausted once I finished with my parents. They had decades more of memories that needed to be filed away. If I didn't have all of Genevieve's and Louis's experiences to draw on, I never would have been able to manage it.

When I was done, the four of us were sitting on my parents' bed, silent.

Mom's and Dad's eyes were back to normal, but they were both stunned, and I could tell they had a ton of questions. I'd given them everything back, after all—from Genevieve stealing their memories to their behavior the past few days when they'd practically forgotten they had children. They hadn't shifted over on the bed to be as far apart from each other as they could be, which is how they normally would have behaved in this setup. Maybe things might change with them after all. Maybe this whole fiasco was what they'd needed to get over their issues.

Or maybe I was dreaming.

"Mom?" I said. "Dad?" I paused for a few seconds, trying to get up the nerve to start. Where to begin? I could tell them about Genevieve and Louis. Tell them about Memory Thieving or about how I'd have to somehow try to restore everyone's memorie's in the town over the next few days. About stealing their anger. Getting their happiness taken away. Kelly and I could confront them about their fight a few nights ago. We could talk about how their fighting terrified us. How the uncertainty of everything was worse than anything else.

But where do you start a conversation like that? How do you do it?

In the end, I had to go with the simple approach. "We need to talk," I said.

And we did.

ACKNOWLEDGEMENTS

First, a huge thank-you to my editor, Jordan Hamessley, for believing enough in this book to buy it not just once, but twice. She went above and beyond the call of duty to help Benji's story see the light of day. Another big round of thanks to my agents, Joshua Bilmes and Eddie Schneider, and all the folks at JABberwocky (particularly Lisa Rodgers, who gave great input early on in the process). They do a spectacular job at everything from career advice to always knowing the right restaurant for any occasion.

I had a veritable slew of readers give me feedback for this book: Lexie Austin, Dantzel Cherry, Megan Grey, Lesley Hart Gunn, Kristina Kugler, Christopher Kugler, Anne Osborne, Bradley Reneer, and Holly Venable. Tomas Cundick has become my go-to reader for all my drafts, and he continues to amaze me with just how fast he can plow through the pages. Daniela and Michaela are pros when it comes to cheering me on. Farrah Keeler did an excellent job selecting names when duty called.

Finally, my wife, Denisa, played a big part in this book. We were on our way to Portland one day when I asked her to help me come up with the idea for a new project, and she delivered in spades.